The
VITAL SPARK
THE ILLUSTRATED PARA HANDY

The VITAL SPARK

THE ILLUSTRATED PARA HANDY

NEIL MUNRO

ILLUSTRATED BY HAMISH HASWELL-SMITH

BLACK & WHITE PUBLISHING

This edition first published in 2003
by Black & White Publishing Ltd
99 Giles Street, Edinburgh EH6 6BZ

ISBN 1 902927 78 8

A CIP catalogue record for this book is available from The British Library.

Printed and bound in Spain by Bookprint S.L., Barcelona

CONTENTS

1

PARA HANDY, MASTER MARINER

A SHORT, thick-set man, with a red beard, a hard round felt hat, ridiculously out of harmony with a blue pilot jacket and trousers and a seaman's jersey, his hands immersed deeply in those pockets our fathers (and the heroes of Rabelais) used to wear behind a front flap, he would have attracted my notice even if he had not, unaware of my presence so close behind him, been humming to himself the chorus of a song that used to be very popular on gabbarts, but is now gone out of date, like "The Captain with the Whiskers took a Sly Glance at Me". You may have heard it thirty years ago, before the steam puffer came in to sweep the sailing smack from all the seas that lie between Bowling and Stornoway. It runs –

"Young Munro he took a notion
  For to sail across the sea,
And he left his true love weeping,
  All alone on Greenock Quay,"

and by that sign, and by his red beard, and by a curious gesture he had, as if he were now and then going to scratch his ear and only determined not to do it when his hand was up, I knew he was one of the Macfarlanes. There were ten Macfarlanes, all men, except one, and he was a valet, but the family did their best to conceal the fact, and said he was away on the yachts, and making that much money he had not time to write a scrape home.

"I think I ought to know you," I said to the vocalist with the hard hat. "You are a Macfarlane: either the Beekan, or Kail, or the Nipper, or Keep Dark, or Para Handy –"

"As sure as daith," said he, "I'm chust Para Handy, and I ken your name fine, but I cannot chust mind your face." He had turned round on the pawl he sat on, without taking his hands from his pockets, and looked up at me where I stood beside him, watching a river steamer being warped into the pier.

"My goodness!" he said about ten minutes later, when he had wormed my whole history out of me; "and you'll be writing things for the papers? Cot bless me! and do you tell me you can be makin' a living off that? I'm not asking you, mind, hoo mich you'll be makin', don't tell me; not a cheep! not a cheep! But I'll wudger it's more than Maclean the munister. But och! I'm not saying: it iss not my business. The munister has two hundred in the year and a coo's gress; he iss aye the big man up yonder, but it iss me would like to show him he wass not so big a man as yourself. Eh? But not a cheep! not a cheep! A Macfarlane would never put his nose into another man's oar."

"And where have you been this long while?" I asked, having let it sink into his mind that there was no chance to-day of his learning my exact income, expenditure, and how much I had in the bank.

"Me!" said he; "I am going up and down like yon fellow in the Scruptures – what wass his name? Sampson – seeking what I may devour. I am out of a chob. Chust that: out of a chob. You'll not be hearin' of anybody in your line that iss in want of a skipper?"

Skippers, I said, were in rare demand in my line of business. We hadn't used a skipper for years.

"Chust that! chust that! I only mentioned it in case. You are making things for newspapers, my Cot! what will they not do now for the penny? Well, that is it; I am out of a chob; chust putting bye the time. I'm not vexed for myself, so mich as for poor Dougie. Dougie wass mate, and I wass skipper. I don't know if you kent the *Fital Spark?*"

The *Vital Spark*, I confessed, was well known to me as the most uncertain puffer that ever kept the Old New-Year in Upper Lochfyne.

"That wass her!" said Macfarlane, almost weeping. "There was never the bate of her, and I have sailed in her four years over twenty with my he'rt in my mooth for fear of her boiler. If you never saw the F*ital Spark,* she is aal hold, with the boiler behind, four men and a derrick, and a watter-butt and a pan loaf in the fo'c'sle. Oh man! she wass the beauty! She was chust sublime! She should be carryin' nothing but gentry for passengers, or nice genteel luggage for the shooting-lodges, but there they would be spoilin' her and rubbin' all the pent off her with their coals, and sand, and whunstone, and oak bark, and timber, and trash like that."

"I understood she had one weakness at least, that her boiler was apt to prime."

"It's a – lie," cried Macfarlane, quite furious; "her boiler never primed more than wance a month, and that wass not with fair play. If Dougie wass here he would tell you.

"I wass ass prood of that boat ass the Duke of Argyll, ay, or Lord Breadalbane. If you would see me waalkin' aboot on her dake when we wass lyin' at the quay! There wasna the like of it in the West Hielan's. I wass chust sublime! She had a gold bead aboot her; it's no lie I am tellin' you, and I would be pentin' her oot of my own pocket every time we went to Arran for gravel. She drawed four feet forrit and nine aft, and she could go like the duvvle."

"I have heard it put at five knots," I said maliciously.

Macfarlane bounded from his seat. "Five knots!" he cried. "Show me the man that says five knots, and I will make him swallow the hatchet. Six knots, ass sure ass my name iss Macfarlane; many a time between the Skate and Otter. If Dougie wass here he would tell you. But I am not braggin' aboot her sailin'; it wass her looks. Man, she was smert, smert! Every time she wass new pented I would be puttin' on my Sunday clothes. There wass a time yonder they would be callin' me Two-flag Peter in Loch Fyne. It wass wance the Queen had a jubilee, and we had but the wan flag, but a Macfarlane never wass bate, and I put up the wan flag and a regatta shirt, and I'm telling you she looked chust sublime!"

"I forget who it was once told me she was very wet," I cooed blandly; "that with a head wind

3

the *Vital Spark* nearly went out altogether. Of course, people will say nasty things about these hookers. They say she was very ill to trim, too."

Macfarlane jumped up again, grinding his teeth, and his face purple. He could hardly speak with indignation. "Trum!" he shouted. "Did you say 'trum'? You could trum her with the wan hand behind your back and you lookin' the other way. To the duvvle with your trum! And they would be sayin' she wass wet! If Dougie wass here he would tell you. She would not take in wan cup of watter unless it wass for synin' oot the dishes. She wass that dry she would not wet a postage stamp unless we slung it over the side in a pail. She wass sublime, chust sublime!

"I am telling you there iss not many men following the sea that could sail the *Fital Spark* the way I could. There iss not a rock, no, nor a chuckie stone inside the Cumbrie Heid that I do not have a name for. I would ken them fine in the dark by the smell, and that iss not easy, I'm telling you. And I am not wan of your dry-land sailors. I wass wance at Londonderry with her. We went at night, and did Dougie no' go away and forget oil, so that we had no lamps, and chust had to sail in the dark with our ears wide open. If Dougie wass here he would tell you. Now and then Dougie would be striking a match for fear of a collusion."

"Where did he show it?" I asked innocently. "Forward or aft?"

"Aft," said the mariner suspiciously. "What for would it be aft? Do you mean to say there could be a collusion aft? I am telling you she could do her six knots before she cracked her shaft. It wass in the bow, of course; Dougie had the matches. She wass chust sublime. A gold bead oot of my own pocket, four men and a derrick, and a watter-butt and a pan loaf in the fo'c'sle. My bonnie wee *Fital Spark*!"

He began to show symptoms of tears, and I hate to see an ancient mariner's tears, so I hurriedly asked him how he had lost the command.

"I will tell you that," said he. "It was Dougie's fault. We had yonder a cargo of coals for Tarbert, and we got doon the length of Greenock, going fine, fine. It wass the day after the New Year, and I wass in fine trum, and Dougie said, 'Wull we stand in here for orders?' and so we went into Greenock for some marmalade, and did we no' stay three days? Dougie and me wass going about

Greenock looking for signboards with Hielan' names on them, and every signboard we could see with Campbell, or Macintyre, on it, or Morrison, Dougie would go in and ask if the man came from Kilmartin or anyway roond aboot there, and if the man said no, Dougie would say, 'It's a great peety, for I have cousins of the same name, but maybe you'll have time to come oot for a dram?' Dougie was chust sublime!

"Every day we would be getting sixpenny telegrams from the man the coals was for at Tarbert, but och! we did not think he wass in such an aawful hurry, and then he came himself to Greenock with the *Grenadier*, and the only wans that wass not in the polis-office wass myself and the derrick. He bailed the laads out of the polis-office, and 'Now,' he said, 'you will chust sail her up as fast as you can, like smert laads, for my customers iss waiting for their coals, and I will go over and see my good-sister at Helensburgh, and go back to Tarbert the day efter to-morrow.' 'Hoo can we be going and us with no money?' said Dougie – man, he wass sublime! So the man gave me a paper pound of money, and went away to Helensburgh, and Dougie wass coilin' up a hawser forrit ready to start from the quay. When he wass away, Dougie said we would maybe chust be as weel to wait another tide, and I said I didna know, but what did he think, and he said, 'Ach, of course!' and we went aal back into Greenock. 'Let me see that pound!' said Dougie, and did I not give it to him? and then he rang the bell of the public hoose we were in, and asked for four tacks and a wee hammer. When he got the four tacks and the wee hammer he nailed the pound note on the door, and said to the man, 'Chust come in with a dram every time we ring the bell till that's done!' If Dougie wass here he would tell you. Two days efter that the owner of the *Fital Spark* came doon from Gleska and five men with him, and they went away with her to Tarbert."

"And so you lost the old command," I said, preparing to go off. "Well, I hope something will turn up soon."

"There wass some talk aboot a dram," said the mariner. "I thought you said something aboot a dram, but och! there's no occasion!"

A week later, I am glad to say, the Captain and his old crew were reinstated on the *Vital Spark*.

2

THE PRIZE CANARY

"CANARIES!" said Para Handy contemptuously, "I have a canary yonder at home that would give you a sore heid to hear him singing. He's chust sublime. Have I no', Dougie?"

It was the first time the mate had ever heard of the Captain as a bird-fancier, but he was a loyal friend, and at Para Handy's wink he said promptly, "You have that, Peter. Wan of the finest ever stepped. Many a sore heid I had wi't."

"What kind of a canary is it?" asked the Brodick man jealously. "Is it a Norwich?"

Para Handy put up his hand as usual to scratch his ear, and checked the act half-way. "No, nor a Sandwich; it's chust a plain yellow wan," he said coolly. "I'll wudger ye a pound it could sing the best you have blin'. It whustles even-on, night and day, till I have to put it under a bowl o' watter if I'm wantin' my night's sleep."

The competitive passions of the Brodick man were roused. He considered that among his dozen prize canaries he had at least one that could beat anything likely to be in the possession of the Captain of the *Vital Spark*, which was lying at Brodick when this conversation took place. He produced it – an emaciated, sickle-shaped, small-headed, bead-eyed, business-looking bird, which he called the Wee Free. He was prepared to put up the pound for a singing contest anywhere in Arran, date hereafter to be arranged.

"That's all right," said Para Handy, "I'll take you on. We'll be doon this way for a cargo of grevel in a week, and if the money's wi' the man in the shippin'-box at the quay, my canary'll lift it."

"But what aboot your pound?" asked the Brodick man. "You must wudger a pound too."

"Is that the way o't?" said the Captain. "I wass never up to the gemblin', but I'll risk the pound," and so the contest was arranged.

"But you havena a canary at aal, have you?" said Dougie, later in the day, as the *Vital Spark* was puffing on her deliberate way to Glasgow.

"Me?" said Para Handy, "I would as soon think of keepin' a hoolet. But och, there's plenty in Gleska if you have the money. From the needle to the anchor. Forbye, I ken a gentleman that breeds canaries; he's a riveter, and if I wass gettin' him in good trum he would maybe give me a lend o' wan. If no', we'll take a dander up to the Bird Market, and pick up a smert wan that'll put the hems on Sandy Kerr's Wee Free. No man wi' any releegion aboot him would caal his canary a Wee Free."

The Captain and the mate of the *Vital Spark* left their noble ship at the wharf that evening – it was a Saturday – and went in quest of the gentleman who bred canaries. He was discovered in the midst of an altercation with his wife which involved the total destruction of all the dishes on the kitchen-dresser, and, with a shrewdness and consideration that were never absent in the Captain, he apologised for the untimely intrusion and prepared to go away. "I see you're busy," he said, looking in on a floor covered with the debris of the delf which this ardent lover of bird life was smashing in order to impress his wife with the fact that he was really annoyed about something – "I see you're busy. Fine, man, fine! A wife need never weary in this hoose – it's that cheery. Dougie and me wass chust wantin' a wee lend of a canary for a day or two, but och, it doesna matter, seein' ye're so throng; we'll chust try the shops."

It was indicative of the fine kindly humanity of the riveter who loved canaries that this one unhesitatingly stopped his labours, having disposed of the last plate, and said, "I couldna dae't, chaps; I wadna trust a canary oot o' the hoose; there's nae sayin' the ill-usage it micht get. It would break my he'rt to ha'e onything gang wrang wi' ony o' my birds."

"Chust that, Wull, chust that!" said Para Handy agreeably. "Your feelings does you credit. I would be awful vexed if you broke your he'rt; it'll soon be the only hale thing left in the hoose. If I wass you, and had such a spite at the delf, I would use dunnymite," and Dougie and he departed.

"That's the sort of thing that keeps me from gettin' merrit," the Captain, with a sigh, confided to his mate, when they got down the stair. "Look at the money it costs for dishes every Setturday night."

"Them riveters iss awfu' chaps for sport," said Dougie irrelevantly.

"There's nothing for't now but the Bird Market," said the Captain, leading the way east along Argyle Street. They had no clear idea where that institution was, but at the corner of Jamaica Street consulted several Celtic compatriots, who put them on the right track. Having reached the Bird Market, the Captain explained his wants to a party who had "Guaranteed A1 Songsters" to sell at two shillings. This person was particularly enthusiastic about one bird which in the meantime was as silent as "the harp that once through Tara's halls". He gave them his solemn assurance it was a genuine prize roller canary; that when it started whistling, as it generally did at breakfast time, it sang till the gas was lit, with not even a pause for refreshment. For that reason it was an economical canary to keep; it practically cost nothing for seed for this canary. If it was a songster suitable for use on a ship that was wanted, he went on, with a rapid assumption that his customers were of a maritime profession, this bird was peculiarly adapted for the post. It was a genuine imported bird, and had already made a sea voyage. To sell a bird of such exquisite parts for two shillings was sheer commercial suicide; he admitted it, but he was anxious that it should have a good home.

"I wish I could hear it whustlin'," said the Captain, peering through the spars at the very dejected bird, which was a moulting hen.

"It never sings efter the gas is lighted," said the vendor regretfully, "that's the only thing that's wrang wi't. If that bird wad sing at nicht when the gas was lit, it wad solve the problem o' perpetual motion."

Para Handy, considerably impressed by this high warrandice, bought the canary, which was removed from the cage and placed in a brown paper sugar-bag, ventilated by holes which the bird-seller made in it with the stub of a lead pencil.

"Will you no' need a cage?" asked Dougie.

"Not at aal, not at aal!" the Captain protested; "wance we get him doon to Brodick we'll get plenty o' cages," and away they went with their purchase, Para Handy elate at the imminent prospect of his prize canary winning an easy pound. Dougie carefully carried the bag containing the bird.

Some days after, the *Vital Spark* arrived at Brodick, but the Captain, who had not yet staked his pound with the man in the shipping-box as agreed on, curiously enough showed no disposition to bring off the challenge meeting between the birds. It was by accident he met the Brodick man one day on the quay.

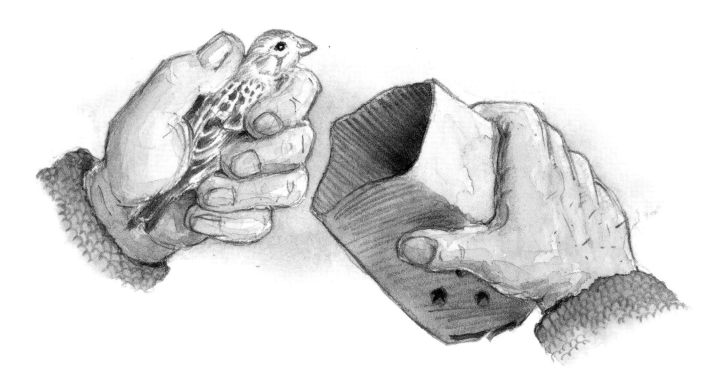

"Talking about birds," said Para Handy, with some diffidence, "Dougie and me had a canary yonder –"

"That's aal off," said the Brodick man hurriedly, getting very red in the face, showing so much embarrassment, indeed, that the Captain of the *Vital Spark* smelt a rat.

"What way off?" he asked. "It sticks in my mind that there wass a kind of a wudger, and that there's a pound note in the shupping-box for the best canary."

"Did you bring your canary?" asked the Brodick man anxiously.

"It's doon there in the vessel singin' like to take the rivets oot o' her," said Para Handy. "It's chust sublime to listen to."

"Weel, the fact iss, I'm not goin' to challenge," said the Brodick man. "I have a wife yonder, and she's sore against bettin' and wudgerin' and gemblin', and she'll no let me take my champion bird Wee Free over the door."

"Chust that!" said Para Handy. "That's a peety. Weel, weel, the pund'll come in handy. I'll chust go away down to the shupping-box and lift it. Seeing I won, I'll stand you a drink."

The Brodick man maintained with warmth that as Para Handy had not yet lodged his stake of a pound the match was off; an excited discussion followed, and the upshot was a compromise. The Brodick man, having failed to produce his bird, was to forfeit ten shillings, and treat the crew of the *Vital Spark*.

They were being treated, and the ten shillings were in Para Handy's possession, when the Brodick sportsman rose to make some disconcerting remark.

"You think you are very smert, Macfarlane," he said, addressing the Captain. "You are thinkin' you did a good stroke to get the ten shullin's, but if you wass smerter it iss not the ten shullin's you would have at aal, but the pound. I had you fine, Macfarlane. My wife never said a word aboot the wudger, but my bird is in the pook, and couldna sing a note this week. That's the way I backed oot."

Para Handy displayed neither resentment nor surprise. He took a deep draught of beer out of a quart pot, and then smiled with mingled tolerance and pity on the Brodick man.

"Ay, ay!" he said, "and you think you have done a smert thing. You have mich caause to be ashamed of yourself. You are nothing better than a common swundler. But och, it doesna matter; the fact iss, oor bird's deid."

"Deid!" cried the Brodick man. "What do you mean by deid?"

"Chust that it's no' livin'," said Para Handy coolly. "Dougie and me bought wan in the Bird Market, and Dougie was carryin' it doon to the vessel in a sugar-poke when he met some fellows he kent in Chamaica Street, and went for a dram, or maybe two. Efter a while he didna mind what he had in the poke, and he put it in his troosers pockets, thinkin' it wass something extra for the Sunday's dinner. When he brought the poor wee bird oot of his pocket in the mornin', it wass chust a' remains."

3

THE MALINGERER

THE crew of the *Vital Spark* were all willing workers, except The Tar, who was usually as tired when he rose in the morning as when he went to bed. He said himself it was his health, and that he had never got his strength right back since he had the whooping-cough twice when he was a boy. The Captain was generally sympathetic, and was inclined to believe The Tar was destined to have a short life unless he got married and had a wife to look after him. "A wife's the very thing for you," he would urge; "it's no' canny, a man as delicate as you to be having nobody to depend on."

"I couldna afford a wife," The Tar always maintained. "They're all too grand for the like of me."

"Och ay! but you might look aboot you and find a wee, no' aawfu' bonny wan," said Para Handy.

"If she was blin', or the like of that, you would have a better chance of gettin' her," chimed in Dougie, who always scoffed at The Tar's periodical illnesses, and cruelly ascribed his lack of energy to sheer laziness.

The unfortunate Tar's weaknesses always seemed to come on him when there was most to do. It generally took the form of sleepiness, so that sometimes when he was supposed to be preparing the dinner he would be found sound asleep on the head of a bucket, with a half-peeled potato in his hand. He once crept out of the fo'c'sle rubbing his eyes after a twelve-hours' sleep, saying, "Tell me this and tell me no more, am I going to my bed or comin' from it?"

But there was something unusual and alarming about the illness which overtook The Tar on their way up Loch Fyne to lift a cargo of timber. First he had shivers all down his back; then he got so stiff that he could not bend to lift a bucket, but had to kick it along the deck in front of him, which made Dougie admiringly say, "Man! you are an aawful handy man with your feet, Colin"; his appetite, he declared, totally disappeared immediately after an unusually hearty breakfast composed of six herrings and two eggs; and finally he expressed his belief that there was nothing for it but his bed.

"I'll maybe no trouble you long, boys," he moaned lugubriously. "My heid's birling roond that fast that I canna even mind my own name two meenutes."

"You should write it on a wee bit paper," said Dougie unfeelingly, "and keep it inside your bonnet, so that you could look it up at any time you were needin'."

Para Handy had kinder feelings, and told The Tar to go and lie down for an hour or two and take a wee drop of something.

"Maybe a drop of brandy would help me," said The Tar, promptly preparing to avail himself of the Captain's advice.

"No, not brandy; a drop of good Brutish spurits will suit you better, Colin," said the Captain, and went below to dispense the prescription himself.

The gusto with which The Tar swallowed the prescribed dram of British spirits and took a chew of tobacco after it to enhance the effect, made Para Handy somewhat suspicious, and he said so to Dougie when he got on deck, leaving The Tar already in a gentle slumber.

"The rascal's chust scheming," said Dougie emphatically. "There iss nothing in the world wrong with him but the laziness. If you'll notice, he aalways gets no weel when we're going to lift timber, because it iss harder on him at the winch."

The Captain was indignant, and was for going down there and then with a rope's-end to rouse the patient, but Dougie confided to him a method of punishing the malingerer and at the same time getting some innocent amusement for themselves.

Dinner-time came round. The Tar instinctively wakened and lay wondering what they would

take down to him to eat. The *Vital Spark* was puff-puffing her deliberate way up the loch, and there was an unusual stillness on deck. It seemed to The Tar that the Captain and Dougie were moving about on tiptoe and speaking in whispers. The uncomfortable feeling this created in his mind was increased when his two shipmates came down with slippers on instead of their ordinary sea-boots, creeping down the companion with great caution, carrying a bowl of gruel.

"What's that for?" asked The Tar sharply. "Are you going to paste up any bills?"

"Wheest, Colin," said Para Handy, in a sick-room whisper. "You must not excite yourself, but take this gruel. It'll do you no herm. Poor fellow, you're looking aawful bad." They hung over his bunk with an attitude of chastened grief, and Dougie made to help him to the gruel with a spoon as if he were unable to feed himself.

"Have you no beef?" asked The Tar, looking at the gruel with disgust. "I'll need to keep up my strength with something more than gruel."

"You daurna for your life take anything but gruel," said the Captain sorrowfully. "It would be the daith of you at wance to take beef, though there's plenty in the pot. Chust take this, like a good laad, and don't speak. My Chove! you are looking far through."

"Your nose is as sherp as a preen," said Dougie in an awed whisper, and with a piece of engine-room waste wiped the brow of The Tar, who was beginning to perspire with alarm.

"I don't think I'm so bad ass aal that," said the patient. "It wass chust a turn; a day in my bed'll put me aal right – or maybe two."

They shook their heads sorrowfully, and the Captain turned away as if to hide a tear. Dougie blew his nose with much ostentation and stifled a sob.

"What's the metter wi' you?" asked The Tar, looking at them in amazement and fear.

"Nothing, nothing, Colin," said the Captain. "Don't say a word. Iss there anything we could get for you?"

"My heid's bad yet," the patient replied. "Perhaps a drop of spurits –"

"There's no' another drop in the ship," said the Captain.

The patient moaned. "And I don't suppose there's any beer either?" he said hopelessly.

He was told there was no beer, and instructed to cry if he was requiring anyone to come to his assistance, after which the two nurses crept quietly on deck again, leaving him in a very uneasy frame of mind.

They got into the quay late in the afternoon, and the Captain and mate came down again quietly, with their caps in their hands, to discover The Tar surreptitiously smoking in his bunk to dull the pangs of hunger that now beset him, for they had given him nothing since the gruel.

"It's not for you, it's not for you at aal, smokin'!" cried Para Handy in horror, taking the pipe out of his hand. "With the trouble you have, smoking drives it in to the he'rt and kills you at wance."

"What trouble do you think it iss?" asked the patient seriously.

"Dougie says it's – it's – what did you say it wass, Dougie?"

"It's convolvulus in the inside," said Dougie solemnly; "I had two aunties that died of it in their unfancy."

"I'm going to get up at wance!" said The Tar, making to rise, but they thrust him back in his blankets, saying the convolvulus would burst at the first effort of the kind he made.

He began to weep. "Fancy a trouble like that coming on me, and me quite young!" he said, pitying himself seriously. "There wass never wan in oor femily had it."

"It's sleep brings it on," said Dougie, with the air of a specialist who would ordinarily charge a fee of ten guineas – "sleep and sitting doon. There iss nothing to keep off convolvulus but exercise and rising early in the morning. Poor fellow! But you'll maybe get better; when there's hope there's life. The Captain and me wass wondering if there wass anything we could buy ashore for you – some grapes, maybe, or a shullin' bottle of sherry wine."

"Mercy on me! am I ass far through ass that?" said The Tar.

"Or maybe you would like Macphail, the enchineer, to come doon and read the Scruptures a while to you," said Para Handy.

"Macphail!" cried the poor Tar; "I wudna let a man like that read a song-book to me."

They clapped him affectionately on the shoulders; Dougie made as if to shake his hand, and checked himself; then the Captain and mate went softly on deck again, and the patient was left with his fears. He felt utterly incapable of getting up.

Para Handy and his mate went up the town and had a dram with the local joiner, who was also undertaker. With this functionary in their company they were moving towards the quay when Dougie saw in a grocer's shop-door a pictorial card bearing the well-known monkey portrait advertising a certain soap that won't wash clothes. He went chuckling into the shop, made some small purchase, and came out the possessor of the picture. Half an hour later, when it was dark, and The Tar was lying in an agony of hunger which he took to be the pains of internal convolvulus, Para Handy, Dougie, and the joiner came quietly down to the fo'c'sle, where he lay. They had no lamp, but they struck matches and looked at him in his bunk with countenances full of pity.

"A nose as sherp as a preen," said Dougie; "it must be the galloping kind of convolvulus."

"Here's Macintyre the joiner would like to see you, Colin," said Para Handy, and in the light of a match the patient saw the joiner cast a rapid professional eye over his proportions.

"What's the joiner wantin' here?" said The Tar, with a frightful suspicion.

"Nothing, Colin, nothing – six by two – I wass chust passing – six by two – chust passing, and the Captain asked me in to see you. It's – six by two, six by two – it's no' very healthy weather we're havin'. Chust that!"

The fo'c'sle was in darkness and The Tar felt already as if he was dead and buried. "Am I lookin' very bad?" he ventured to ask Dougie.

"Bad's no' the name for it," said Dougie. "Chust look at yourself in the enchineer's looking-gless." He produced from under his arm the engineer's little mirror, on the face of which he had gummed the portrait of the monkey cut out from the soap advertisement, which fitted neatly into the frame. The Captain struck a match, and in its brief and insufficient light The Tar looked at himself, as he thought, reflected in the glass.

"Man, I'm no' that awful changed either; if I had a shave and my face washed. I don't believe it's convolvulus at aal," said he, quite hopefully, and jumped from his bunk.

For the rest of the week he put in the work of two men.

4

WEE TEENY

THE last passenger steamer to sail that day from Ardrishaig was a trip from Rothesay. It was Glasgow Fair Saturday, and Ardrishaig Quay was black with people. There was a marvellously stimulating odour of dulse, herring, and shell-fish, for everybody carried away in a handkerchief a few samples of these marine products that are now the only seaside souvenirs not made in Germany. The *Vital Spark*, in ballast, Clydeward bound, lay inside the passenger steamer, ready to start when the latter had got under weigh, and Para Handy and his mate meanwhile sat on the fo'c'sle-head of "the smertest boat in the tred" watching the frantic efforts of lady excursionists to get their husbands on the steamer before it was too late, and the deliberate efforts of the said husbands to slink away up the village again just for one more drink. Wildly the steamer hooted from her siren, fiercely clanged her bell, vociferously the Captain roared upon his bridge, people aboard yelled eagerly to friends ashore to hurry up, and the people ashore as eagerly demanded to know what all the hurry was about, and where the bleezes was Wull. Women loudly defied the purser to let the ship go away without their John, for he had paid his money for his ticket, and though he was only a working man his money was as good as anybody else's; and John, on the quay, with his hat thrust back on his head, his thumbs in the armholes of his waistcoat and a red handkerchief full of dulse at his feet, gave a display of step-dancing that was responsible for a great deal of the congestion of traffic at the shore end of the gangway.

Among the crowd who had got on board was a woman with eleven children. She was standing on the paddle-box counting them to make sure – five attached to the basket that had contained their food for the day, other four clinging to her gown, and one in her arms. "Yin, twa, three, fower, and fower's eight, and twa's ten, and then there's Wee Teeny wi' her faither doon the caibin." She was quite serene. If she could have seen that the father – at that moment in the foresaloon singing

"In the guid auld summer time,

In the guid auld summer time,

She'll be your tootsy-wootsy

In the guid auld summer time."

had no Wee Teeny with him, she would have been distracted. As it was, however, the steamer was miles on her way when a frantic woman with ten crying children all in a row behind her, and a husband miraculously sobered, made a vain appeal to the Captain to go back to Ardrishaig for her lost child.

The child was discovered on the quay by the local police ten minutes after the excursion steamer had started, and just when Para Handy was about to cast off the pawls. She was somewhere about three years old, and the only fact that could be extracted from her was that her name was Teeny. There had probably not been a more contented and self-possessed person on Ardrishaig Quay that day: she sucked her thumb with an air of positive relish, smiled on the slightest provocation, and showed the utmost willingness to go anywhere with anybody.

"The poor wee cratur!" said Para Handy sympathetically. "She minds me fearfully of my brother Cherlie's twuns. I wudna wonder but she'a twuns too; that would be the way the mistake would be made in leavin' her; it's such a terrible thing drink. I'm no' goin' to ask you, Dougie, to do anything you wudna like, but what would you be sayin' to us takin' the wean wi' us and puttin' her ashore at Rothesay? Mind you, chust if you like yoursel'."

"It's your own vessel, you're the skipper of her, and I'm sure and I have no objections, at aal at

aal," said Dougie quite heartily, and it was speedily arranged with the police that a telegram should be sent to wait the Captain of the excursion steamer at Rothesay, telling him the lost child was following in the steam-lighter *Vital Spark*.

Macphail the engineer, and The Tar, kept the child in amusement with pocket-knives, oil-cans, cotton-waste, and other maritime toys, while the Captain and Dougie went hurriedly up the village for stores for the unexpected passenger.

"You'll not need that mich," was Dougie's opinion; "she'll fall asleep as soon as it's dark, and no' wake till we put her ashore at Rothesay."

"Ah, but you canna be sure o' them at that age," said the Captain. "My brother Cherlie wass merrit on a low-country woman, and the twuns used to sit up at night and greet in the two languages, Gaalic and Gleska, till he had to put plugs in them."

"God bless me! plugs?" said Dougie astonished.

"Ay, chust plugs," said the Captain emphatically. "You'll see them often. They're made of kahouchy, with a bone ring on them for screwing them on and off. It's the only thing for stopping them greetin'."

The adventures of Wee Teeny from this stage may be better told as Para Handy told it to me some time afterwards.

"To let you ken," he said, "I wass feared the wean would sterve. Nothing in the ship but sea biscuits and salt beef. I went into wan shop and got a quart of milk on draught, half a pound of boiled ham the same as they have at funerals, and a tin tinny For a Good Girl. Dougie wasna slack either; he went into another shop and got thruppence worth of sweeties and a jumpin'-jeck. It wass as nice a thing ass ever you saw to see the wee cratur sittin' on the hatches eatin' away and drinkin' wi' the wan hand, and laughing like anything at the jumpin'-jeck wi' the other. I never saw the ship cheerier; it wass chust sublime. If Dougie wass here himsel' he would tell you. Everything wass going first-rate, and I wass doon below washing my face and puttin' on my other jecket and my watch-chain oot o' respect for the passenger, when Dougie came doon in a hurry wi' a long face on him, and says –

" 'She's wantin' ta-ta.'

" 'Mercy on us, she canna be more ta-ta than she iss unless we throw her over the side,' I says to Dougie. But I went up on dake and told her she would be ta-ta in no time becaase the ship was loggin' six knots and the wind wi' us.

" 'Ta-ta,' says she, tuggin' my whuskers the same as if I wass merrit on her – ah, man! she wass a nice wee thing. And that good-natured! The best I could do wass to make The Tar show her the tattoo marks on his legs, and Dougie play the trump (Jew's harp), and when she wass tired o' that I carried her up and doon the dake singin' 'Auld Lang Syne' till she was doverin' over.

" 'She's goin' to sleep noo,' I says to Dougie, and we put her in my bunk wi' her clothes on. She wanted her clothes off, but I said, 'Och! never mind puttin' them off, Teeny; it's only a habit.' Dougie said, if he minded right, they always put up a kind of prayer at that age. 'Give her a start,' I says to Dougie, and he said the 23rd Psalm in Gaalic, but she didn't understand wan word of it, and went to sleep wi' a poke o' sweeties in her hand.

"We were off Ardlamont, and Macphail wass keepin' the boat bangin' at it to get to Rothesay before the mother went oot of her wuts, when I heard a noise doon below where Teeny wass. I ran doon and found her sittin' up chokin' wi' a sweetie that wass a size too lerge for her. She wass black in the face.

" 'Hut her on the back, Peter!' said Dougie.

" 'Hut her yoursel'; I wudna hurt her for the world,' I says, and Dougie said he wudna do it either, but he ran up for The Tar, that hasna mich feelin's, and The Tar saved her life. I'm tellin' you it wass a start! We couldna trust her below, herself, efter that, so we took her on dake again. In ten meenutes she fell down among Macphail's engines, and nearly spoiled them. She wasna hurt a bit, but Macphail's feelin's wass, for she wass wantin' the engines to her bed wi' her. She thought they were a kind of a toy. We aye keep that up on him yet.

" 'My Chove! this wean's no' canny,' said Dougie, and we took her up on dake again, and put up the sail to get as mich speed oot of the vessel as we could for Rothesay. Dougie played the trump even-on to her, and The Tar walked on his hands till she was sore laughing at him. Efter a bit we took oor eyes off her for maybe two meenutes, and when we turned roond again Teeny wass fallin' doon into the fo'c'sle.

" 'This iss the worst cargo ever we had,' I says, takin' her up again no' a bit the worse. 'If we don't watch her like a hawk aal the time she'll do something desperate before we reach Rothesay. She'll jump over the side or crawl doon the funnel, and we'll be black affronted.'

" 'I wudna say but you're right,' said Dougie. We put her sittin' on the hatch wi' the jumpin'-jeck, and the tin tinny For a Good Girl, and my watch and chain, Dougie's trump, the photygraph of The Tar's lass, and Macphail's new carpet sluppers to play wi', and the three of us sat roond her watchin' she didna swallow the watch and chain.

"When I handed her over to her mother and father on Rothesay Quay, I says to them, 'I'm gled I'm no' a mother; I would a hunder times sooner be a sailor.'

"But it's a nice thing a wean, too; for a week efter that we missed her awful," concluded the Captain pensively.

5

THE MATE'S WIFE

THAT the Captain of the *Vital Spark* should so persistently remain a bachelor surprised many people. He was just the sort of man, in many respects, who would fall an easy prey to the first woman on the look-out for a good home. He had rather a gallant way with the sex, generally said "mem" to them all, regardless of class; liked their society when he had his Sunday clothes on, and never contradicted them. If he had pursued any other calling than that of mariner I think he would have been captured long ago; his escape doubtless lay in the fact that sailing about from place to place, only briefly touching at West-Coast quays, and then being usually grimed with coal-dust, he had never properly roused their interest and natural sporting instincts. They never knew what a grand opportunity they were losing.

"I'm astonished you never got married, Captain," I said to him recently.

"Ach, I couldn't be bothered," he replied, like a man who had given the matter his consideration before now. "I'm that busy wi' the ship I havena time. There's an aawful lot of bother aboot a wife. Forbye, my he'rt's in the *Fital Spark* – there's no' a smerter boat in the tred. Wait you till I get her pented!"

"But a ship's not a wife, Captain," I protested.

"No," said he, "but it's a responsibility. You can get a wife any time that'll stick to you the same as if she wass riveted as long's you draw your pay, but it takes a man with aal his senses aboot him to get a ship and keep her. And chust think on the expense! Oh, I'm not sayin', mind you, that I'll not try wan some day, but there's no hurry, no, not a bit."

"But perhaps you'll put it off too long," I said, "and when you're in the humour to have them they won't have you."

He laughed at the very idea.

"Man!" he said, "it's easy seen you have not studied them. I ken them like the Kyles of Bute. The captain of a steamer iss the most popular man in the wide world – popularer than the munisters themselves, and the munisters iss that popular the weemen put bird-lime in front of the Manses to catch them, the same ass if they were green-linties. It's worse with sea-captains – they're that dashing, and they're not aalways hinging aboot the hoose wi' their sluppers on."

"There's another thing," he added, after a little pause, "I couldna put up with a woman comin' aboot the vessel every pay-day. No, no, I'm for none o' that. Dougie's wife's plenty."

"But surely she does not invade you weekly?" I said, surprised.

"If the *Fital Spark's* anywhere inside Ardlamont on a Setturday," said Para Handy, "she's doon wi' the first steamer from Gleska, and her door-key in her hand, the same ass if it wass a pistol to put to his heid. If Dougie was here himsel' he would tell you. She's a low-country woman, wi' no' a word o' Gaalic, so that she canna understand Dougie at his best. When it comes to bein' angry in English, she can easy bate him. Oh, a cluvver woman: she made Dougie a Rechabite, and he's aalways wan when he's at home, and at keepin' him trum and tidy in his clothes she's chust sublime. But she's no' canny aboot a ship. The first week after she married him we were lyin' at Innellan, and doon she came on the Setturday wi' her door-key at full cock. When Dougie saw her comin' doon the quay he got white, and turned to me, sayin', 'Peter, here's the Mustress; I wish I hadna touched that dram, she'll can tell it on me, and I'm no' feared for her, but it would hurt her feelings.'

" 'Man!' I said, ' you're an aawful tumid man for a sailor; but haste you doon the fo'c'sle and you'll get a poke of peppermint sweeties in my other pocket I had for the church to-morrow. Chust you go like the duvvle, and I'll keep her in conversation till you get your breath shifted.'

"Dougie bolted doon below, and wass up in a shot. 'I got the sweeties, Peter,' he said, 'but, oh! she's as cunning as a jyler, and she'll chalouse something if she smells the peppermints. What would you say to the whole of us takin' wan or two sweeties so that we would be aal the same, and she wouldna suspect me?' 'Very weel,' I said, 'anything to obleege a mate,' and when the good leddy reached the side of the vessel the enchineer and The Tar and me and Dougie wass standin' in a row eating peppermints till you would think it wass the front sate of the Tobermory Free Church.

" 'It's a fine day and an awfu' smell o' losengers,' was the first words she said when she put her two feet on the deck. And she looked very keen at her man.

" 'It is that, mem,' I said. 'It's the cargo.'

" 'What cargo?' said she, looking at Dougie harder than ever. 'I'll cargo him!' "

" 'I mean the cargo of the boat, mem,' I said quite smert. 'It's a cheneral cargo, and there's six ton of peppermint sweeties for the Tarbert fishermen.'

" 'What in the wide world dae the Tarbert fishermen dae wi' sae mony sweeties?' said she.

" 'Och, it's chust to keep them from frightening away the herrin' when they're oot at the fishin',' I said. Man! I'm tellin' you I had aal my wuts aboot me that day! It wass lucky for us the hatches wass doon, so that she couldna see the cargo we had in the hold. There wasna wan sweetie in it.

"I couldna but be nice to the woman, for she wasna my wife, so I turned a bucket upside doon and gave her a sate, and let on that Dougie was chust ass mich a man of consequence on the *Fital Spark* as myself. It does not do to let a wife see wi' her own eyes that her man iss under you in your chob, for when she'll get him at home she'll egg him on to work harder and get your place, and where are you then, eh! where are you then, I'm asking? She wass a cluvver woman, but she had no sense. 'Weel,' said she, 'I don't think muckle o' yer boat. I thocht it was a great big boat, wi' a cabin in it. Instead o' that, it's jist a wee coal yin.'

"Man! do you know that vexed me; I say she wasna the kind of woman Dougie should have married at aal, at aal. Dougie's a chentleman like mysel'; he would never hurt your feelings unless he was tryin'.

" 'There's nothing wrong with the *Fital Spark*, mem,' I said to her. 'She's the most namely ship in the tred; they'll be writing things aboot her in the papers, and men often come to take photographs of her.'

"She chust sniffed her nose at that, the way merrit women have, and said, 'Jist fancy that!'

" 'Yes; chust fancy it!' I said to her. 'Six knots in a gale of wind if Macphail the enchineer is in good trum, and maybe seven if it's Setturday, and him in a hurry to get home. She has the finest lines of any steamboat of her size coming oot of Clyde; if her lum wass pented yellow and she had a bottom strake or two of green, you would take her for a yat. Perhaps you would be thinkin' we should have a German band on board of her, with the heid fuddler goin' aboot gaitherin' pennies in a shell, and the others keekin' over the ends of their flutes and cornucopias for fear he'll pocket some. What? H'm! Chust that!'

"Efter a bit she said she would like to see what sort of place her man and the rest of us slept in, so there was nothing for it but to take her doon to the fo'c'sle, though it wass mich against my will. When she saw the fo'c'sle she wass nestier than ever. She said, 'Surely this iss not a place for Christian men'; and I said, 'No, mem, but we're chust sailors.'

" 'There's nae richt furniture in't,' she said.

" 'Not at present, mem,' I said. 'Perhaps you were expectin' a piano,' but, och! she wass chust wan of them Gleska women, she didna know life. She went away up the toon there and then, and came back wi' a bit of waxcloth, a tin of black soap, a grocer's calendar, and a wee lookin'-gless, hung her bonnet and the door-key on a cleat, and started scrubbin' oot the fo'c'sle. Man, it wass chust peetiful! There wass a damp smell in the fo'c'sle I could feel for months efter, and I had a cold in my heid for a fortnight. When she had the floor of the fo'c'sle scrubbed, she laid the bit of waxcloth, got two nails from The Tar, and looked for a place to hang up the calendar and the wee lookin'-gless, though there wass not mich room for ornaments of the kind. 'That's a little mair tidy-like,' she said when she was feenished, and she came up lookin' for something else to wash. The Tar saw the danger and went ashore in a hurry.

" 'Are ye merrit?' she asked me before she left the vessel wi' Dougie's pay.

" 'No, mem,' I said, 'I'm not merrit yet.'

" 'I could easy see that,' she said, sniffin' her nose again, the same ass if I wass not a captain at aal, but chust before the mast. 'I could easy see that. It's time you were hurryin' up. I ken the very wife wad suit you; she's a kizzen o' my ain, a weedow wumman no' a bit the worse o' the wear.'

" 'Chust that!' said I, 'but I'm engaged.'

" 'Wha to?' she asked quite sherp, no' very sure o' me.

" 'To wan of the Maids of Bute, mem,' I told her, meanin' yon two pented stones you see from the steamer in the Kyles of Bute; and her bein' a Gleska woman, and not traivelled mich, she thocht I wass in earnest.

" 'I don't ken the faimily,' she said, 'but it's my opeenion you wad be better wi' a sensible weedow.'

" 'Not at aal, mem,' I said, 'a sailor couldna have a better wife nor wan of the Maids of Bute; he'll maybe no' get mich tocher with her, but she'll no' come huntin' the quays for him or his wages on the Setturday.' "

6

PARA HANDY – POACHER

THE *Vital Spark* was lying at Greenock with a cargo of scrap-iron, on the top of which was stowed loosely an extraordinary variety of domestic furniture, from bird cages to cottage pianos. Para Handy had just had the hatches off when I came to the quay-side, and he was contemplating the contents of his hold with no very pleasant aspect.

"Rather a mixed cargo!" I ventured to say.

"Muxed's no' the word for't," he said bitterly. "It puts me in mind of an explosion. It's a flittin' from Dunoon. There would be no flittin's in the *Fital Spark* if she wass my boat. But I'm only the captain, och aye! I'm only the captain, thirty-five shullin's a-week and liberty to put on a pea-jecket. To be puttin' scrap-iron and flittin's in a fine smert boat like this iss carryin' coals aboot in a coach and twice. It would make any man use Abyssinian language."

"Abyssinian language?" I repeated, wondering.

"Chust that, Abyssinian language – swearing, and the like of that, you ken fine, yoursel', withoot me tellin' you. Fancy puttin' a flittin' in the *Fital Spark*! You would think she wass a coal-laary, and her with two new coats of pent out of my own pocket since the New Year."

"Have you been fishing?" I asked, desirous to change the subject, which was, plainly, a sore one with the Captain. And I indicated a small fishing-net which was lying in the bows.

"Chust the least wee bit touch," he said, with a very profound wink. "I have a bit of a net there no' the size of a pocket-naipkin, that I use noo and then at the river-mooths. I chust put it doon – me and Dougie – and whiles a salmon or a sea-troot meets wi' an accident and gets into't. Chust a small bit of a net, no' worth speakin' aboot, no' mich bigger nor a pocket-naipkin. They'll be calling it a splash-net, you ken yoursel' withoot me tellin' you." And he winked knowingly again.

"Ah, Captain!" I said, "that's bad! Poaching with a splash-net! I didn't think you would have done it."

"It's no' me; it's Dougie," he retorted promptly. "A fair duvvle for high jeenks, you canna keep him from it. I told him many a time that it wasna right, becaause we might be found oot and get the jyle for't, but he says they do it on aal the smertest yats. Yes, that iss what he said to me – 'They do it on aal the first-cless yats; you'll be bragging the *Fital Spark* iss chust ass good ass any yat, and what for would you grudge a splash-net?' "

"Still it's theft, Captain," I insisted. "And it's very, very bad for the rivers."

"Chust that!" he said complacently. "You'll likely be wan of them fellows that goes to the hotels for the fushing in the rivers. There's more sport aboot a splash-net; if Dougie wass here he would tell you."

"I don't see where the sport comes in," I remarked, and he laughed contemptuously.

"Sport!" he exclaimed. "The best going. There wass wan time yonder we were up Loch Fyne on a Fast Day, and no' a shop open in the place to buy onything for the next mornin's breakfast. Dougie says to me, 'What do you think yoursel' aboot takin' the punt and the small bit of net no' worth mentionin', and going doon to the river mooth when it's dark and seeing if we'll no' get a fush?'

" 'It's a peety to be poaching on the Fast Day,' I said to him.

" 'But it's no' the Fast Day in oor parish,' he said. 'We'll chust give it a trial, and if there's no fush at the start we'll come away back again.' Oh! a consuderate fellow, Dougie; he saw my poseetion at wance, and that I wasna awfu' keen to be fushin' wi' a splash-net on the Fast Day. The end and the short of it wass that when it wass dark we took the net and the punt and rowed doon to the river and began to splash. We had got a fine haul at wance of six great big salmon, and every

salmon Dougie would be takin' oot of the net he would be feeling it all over in a droll way, till I said to him, 'What are you feel-feelin' for, Dougie, the same ass if they had pockets on them? I'm sure they're all right.'

" 'Oh, yes,' he says, 'right enough, but I wass frightened they might be the laird's salmon, and I wass lookin' for the luggage label on them. There's none. It's all right; they're chust wild salmon that nobody planted.'

"Weel, we had got chust ass many salmon ass we had any need for when somebody birled a whustle, and the river watchers put off in a small boat from a point outside of us to catch us. There wass no gettin' oot of the river mooth, so we left the boat and the net and the fush and ran ashore, and by-and-by we got up to the quay and on board the *Fital Spark*, and paaused and consudered things.

" 'They'll ken it's oor boat,' said Dougie, and his clothes wass up to the eyes in salmon scales.

" 'There's no doo't aboot that,' I says. 'If it wassna the Fast Day I wouldna be so vexed; it'll be an awful disgrace to be found oot workin' a splash-net on the Fast Day. And it's a peety aboot the boat, it wass a good boat, I wish we could get her back.'

" 'Ay, it's a peety we lost her,' said Dougie; 'I wonder in the wide world who could have stole her when we were doon the fo'c'sle at oor supper?' Oh, a smert fellow, Dougie! when he said that I saw at wance what he meant.

" 'I'll go up this meenute and report it to the polis office,' I said quite firm, and Dougie said he would go with me too, but that we would need to change oor clothes, for they were covered with fush-scales. We changed oor clothes and went up to the sercheant of polis, and reported that somebody had stolen oor boat.

He wass sittin' readin' his Bible, it bein' the Fast Day, wi' specs on, and he keeked up at us, and said, 'You are very spruce, boys, with your good clothes on at this time of the night.'

" 'We aalways put on oor good clothes on the *Fital Spark* on a Fast Day,' I says to him; 'it's as little as we can do, though we don't belong to the parish.'

"Next day there wass a great commotion in the place aboot some blackguards doon at the river mooth poachin' with a splash-net. The Factor wass busy, and the heid gamekeeper wass busy, and the polis wass busy. We could see them from the dake of the *Fital Spark* goin' aboot buzzin' like bum-bees.

" 'Stop you!' said Dougie to me aal of a sudden. 'They'll be doon here in a chiffy, and findin' us with them scales on oor clothes – we'll have to put on the Sunday wans again.'

" 'But they'll smell something if they see us in oor Sunday clothes,' I said. 'It's no' the Fast Day the day.'

" 'Maybe no' here,' said Dougie, 'but what's to hinder it bein' the Fast Day in oor own parish?'

"We put on oor Sunday clothes again, and looked the Almanac to see if there wass any word in it of a Fast Day any place that day, but there wass nothing in the Almanac but tides, and the Battle of Waterloo, and the weather for next winter. That's the worst of Almanacs; there's nothing in them you want. We were fair bate for a Fast Day any place, when The Tar came up and asked me if he could get to the funeral of a cousin of his in the place at two o'clock.

" 'A funeral!' said Dougie. 'The very thing. The Captain and me'll go to the funeral too. That's the way we have on oor Sunday clothes.' Oh, a smert, smert fellow, Dougie!

"We had chust made up oor mind it wass the funeral we were dressed for, and no' a Fast Day any place, when the polisman and the heid gamekeeper came doon very suspeecious, and said they had oor boat. 'And what's more,' said the gamekeeper, 'there's a splash-net and five stone of salmon in it. It hass been used, your boat, for poaching.'

" 'Iss that a fact?' I says. 'I hope you'll find the blackguards,' and the gamekeeper gave a grunt, and said somebody would suffer for it, and went away busier than ever. But the polis sercheant stopped behind. 'You're still in your Sunday clothes, boys,' said he; 'what iss the occasion to-day?'

" 'We're going to the funeral,' I said.

" 'Chust that! I did not know you were untimate with the diseased,' said the sercheant.

" 'Neither we were,' I said, 'but we are going oot of respect for Colin.' And we went to the funeral, and nobody suspected nothin', but we never got back the boat, for the gamekeeper wass chust needin' wan for a brother o' his own. Och, ay! there's wonderful sport in a splash-net."

7

THE SEA COOK

THE TAR'S duties included cooking for the ship's company. He was not exactly a chef who would bring credit to a first-class club or restaurant, but for some time after he joined the *Vital Spark* there was no occasion to complain of him. Quite often he would wash the breakfast-cups to have them clean for tea in the evening, and it was only when in a great hurry he dried plates with the ship's towel. But as time passed, and he found his shipmates not very particular about what they ate, he grew a little careless. For instance, Para Handy was one day very much annoyed to see The Tar carry forward the potatoes for dinner in his cap.

"That's a droll way to carry potatoes, Colin," he said mildly.

"Och! they'll do no herm; it's only an old kep anyway," said The Tar. "Catch me usin' my other kep for potatoes!"

"It wass not exactly your kep I wass put aboot for," said the Captain. "It wass chust running in my mind that maybe some sort of a dish would be nater and genteeler. I'm no' compleenin', mind you, I'm chust mentioning it."

"Holy smoke!" said The Tar. "You're getting to be aawful polite wi' your plates for potatoes, and them no peeled!"

But the want of variety in The Tar's cooking grew worse and worse each voyage, and finally created a feeling of great annoyance to the crew. It was always essence of coffee and herring –

fresh, salt, kippered, or red – for breakfast, sausages or stewed steak and potatoes for dinner, and a special treat in the shape of ham and eggs for Sundays. One unlucky day for the others of the crew, however, he discovered the convenience of tinned corned beef, and would feed them on that for dinner three or four days a week. Of course they commented on this prevalence of tinned food, which the engineer with some humour always called "malleable mule", but The Tar had any number of reasons ready for its presence on the midday board.

"Sorry, boys," he would say affably, "but this is the duvvle of a place; no' a bit of butcher meat to be got in't till Wednesday, when it comes wi' the boat from Gleska." Or "The fire went oot on me, chaps, chust when I wass making a fine thing. Wait you till Setturday, and we'll have something rare!"

"Ay, ay; live, old horse, and you'll get corn," the Captain would say under these circumstances, as he artistically carved the wedge of American meat. "It's a mercy to get anything; back in your plate, Dougie."

It became at last unbearable, and while The Tar was ashore one day in Tarbert, buying bottled coffee and tinned meat in bulk, a conference between the captain, the engineer, and the mate took place.

"I'm no' going to put up wi't any longer," said the engineer emphatically. "It's all very well for them that has no thinking to do wi' their heids to eat tinned mule even on, but an engineer that's thinking aboot his engines all the time, and sweatin' doon in a temperature o' 120, needs to keep his strength up."

"What sort o' heid-work are you talking aboot?" said the Captain. "Iss it readin' your penny novelles? Hoo's Lady Fitzgerald's man gettin' on?" This last allusion was to Macphail's passion for penny fiction, and particularly to a novelette story over which the engineer had once been foolish enough some years before to show great emotion.

"I move," said Dougie, breaking in on what promised to be an unprofitable altercation, – "I move that The Tar be concurred."

"Concurred!" said the engineer, with a contemptuous snort. "I suppose you mean censured?"

"It's the same thing, only spelled different," said the mate.

"What's censured?" asked the Captain.

"It's giving a fellow a duvvle of a clourin'," answered Dougie promptly.

"No, no, I wouldna care to do that to The Tar. Maybe he's doin' the best he can, poor chap. The Tar never saw mich high life before he came on my boat, and we'll have to make an allowance for that."

"Herrin' for breakfast seven days a week! it's a fair scandal," said the engineer. "If you were maister in your own boat, Macfarlane, you would have a very different kind of man makin' your meat for you."

"There's not mich that iss wholesomer than a good herrin'," said Para Handy. "It's a fush that's chust sublime. But I'll not deny it would be good to have a change noo and then, if it wass only a finnen haddie."

"I have a cookery book o' the wife's yonder at home I'll bring wi' me the next time we're in Gleska, and it'll maybe give him a tip or two," said the engineer, and this was, in the meantime, considered the most expedient thing to do.

Next trip, on the way to Brodick on a Saturday with a cargo of bricks, The Tar was delicately approached by the Captain, who had the cookery book in his hand. "That wass a nice tender bit of tinned beef we had the day, Colin," he said graciously. "Capital, aalthegither! I could live myself on tinned beef from wan end of the year to the other, but Dougie and the enchineer there's compleenin' that you're givin' it to them too often. You would think they were lords! But perhaps I shouldna blame them, for the doctor told the enchineer he should take something tasty every day, and Dougie's aye frightened for tinned meat since ever he heard that the enchineer wance killed a man in the Australian bush. What do you say yoursel' to tryin' something fancy in the cookery line?"

"There's some people hard to please," said The Tar; "I'm sure I'm doin' the best I can to satisfy you aal. Look at them red herrin's I made this mornin'!"

"They were chust sublime!" said the Captain, clapping him on the back. "But chust try a change

to keep their mooths shut. It'll only need to be for a little, for they'll soon tire o' fancy things. I have a kind of a cookery book here you might get some tips in. It's no' mine, mind you, it's Macphail's."

The Tar took the cookery book and turned over some pages with contemptuous and horny fingers.

"A lot o' nonsense!" he said. "Listen to this: 'Take the remains of any cold chicken, mix with the potatoes, put in a pie-dish, and brown with a salamander.' Where are you to get the cold chucken? and where are you to take it? Fancy callin' it a remains; it would be enough to keep you from eatin' chucken. And what's a salamander? There's no' wan on this vessel, at any rate."

"It's chust another name for cinnamon, but you could leave it oot," said the Captain.

"Holy smoke! listen to this," proceeded The Tar: " 'How to make clear stock. Take six or seven pounds of knuckle of beef or veal, half a pound of ham or bacon, a quarter of a pound of butter, two onions, one carrot, one turnip, half a head of salary, and two gallons of water.' You couldna sup that in a week."

"Smaal quantities, smaal quantities, Colin," explained the Captain. "I'm sorry to put you to bother, but there's no other way of pleasin' them other fellows."

"There's no' a thing in this book I would eat except a fowl that's described here," said The Tar, after a further glance through the volume.

"The very thing!" cried the Captain, delighted. "Try a fowl for Sunday," and The Tar said he would do his best.

"I soon showed him who wass skipper on this boat," said the Captain going aft to Dougie and the engineer. "It's to be fowls on Sunday."

There was an old-fashioned cutter yacht at anchor in Brodick Bay with a leg of mutton and two plucked fowls hanging openly under the overhang of her stern, which is sometimes even yet the only pantry a yacht of that type has, though the result is not very decorative.

"Look at that!" said the engineer to The Tar as the *Vital Spark* puffed past the yacht. "There's sensible meat for sailors; no malleable mule. I'll bate you them fellows has a cook wi' aal his wuts aboot him."

"It's aal right, Macphail," said The Tar; "chust you wait till to-morrow and I'll give you fancy cookin'."

And sure enough on Sunday he had two boiled fowls for dinner. It was such an excellent dinner that even the engineer was delighted.

"I'll bate you that you made them hens ready oot o' the wife's cookery book," he said. "There's no' a better cookery book on the South-side of Gleska; the genuine Aunt Kate's. People come far and near for the lend o' that when they're havin' anything extra."

"Where did you buy the hens?" inquired the Captain, nibbling contentedly at the last bone left after the repast.

"I didna buy them at aal," said The Tar. "I couldna be expected to buy chuckens on the money you alloo me. Forbye, it doesna say anything aboot buying in Macphail's cookery book. It says, 'Take two chickens and boil slowly.' So I chust had to take them."

"What do you mean by that?" asked Para Handy, with great apprehension.

"I chust went oot in a wee boat late last night and took them from the stern o' yon wee yacht," said The Tar coolly; and a great silence fell upon the crew of the *Vital Spark*.

"To-morrow," said the Captain emphatically at last – "to-morrow you'll have tinned meat; do you know that, Colin? And you'll never have chucken on the boat again, not if Macphail was breakin' his he'rt for it."

8

LODGERS ON A HOUSE-BOAT

A MAN and his wife came down Crarae Quay from the village. The man carried a spotted yellow tin box in one hand and a bottle of milk in the other. He looked annoyed at something. His wife had one child in her arms, and another walked weeping behind her, occasionally stopping the weeping to suck a stalk of The Original Crarae Rock. There was a chilly air of separation about the little procession that made it plain there had been an awful row. At the quay the *Vital Spark* lay with her hold half covered by the hatches, after discharging a cargo. Her gallant commander, with Dougie, stood beside the winch and watched the family coming down the quay.

"Take my word for it, Dougie," said Para Handy, "that man's no' in very good trum; you can see by the way he's banging the box against his legs and speaking to himsel'. It's no' a hymn he's going over, I'll bate you. And hersel's no' mich better, or she wouldna be lettin' the poor fellow carry the box."

The man came forward to the edge of the quay, looked at the newly painted red funnel of the *Vital Spark*, and seemed, from his countenance, to have been seized by some bright idea.

"Hey! you with the skipped kep," he cried down eagerly to Dougie, "when does this steamer start?"

Para Handy looked at his mate with a pride there was no concealing. "My Chove! Dougie," he said in a low tone to him. "My Chove! he thinks we're opposeetion to the *Lord of the Isles* or the *King Edward*. I'm aye tellin' you this boat iss built on smert lines; if you and me had brass buttons we could make money carryin' passengers."

"Are ye deaf?" cried the man on the quay impatiently, putting down the tin box, and rubbing the sweat from his brow. "When does this boat start?"

"This iss not a boat that starts at aal," said the Captain. "It's a – it's a kind of a yat."

"Dalmighty!" exclaimed the man, greatly crestfallen, "that settles it. I thocht we could get back to Gleska wi' ye. We canna get ludgin's in this place, and whit the bleezes are we to dae when we canna get ludgin's?"

"That's a peety," said the Captain. "It's no' a very nice thing to happen on a Setturday, and there's no way you can get oot of Crarae till Monday unless you have wan of them motor cars."

"We havena oors wi' us," said the wife, taking up a position beside her husband and the tin box. "I'm vexed the only thing o' the kind I ha'e's a cuddy, and if it wasna for him we would ha'e stayed at Rothesay, whaur you can aye get ludgin's o' some kind. Do ye no' think ye could gie us twa nicht's ludgin's on your boat? I'm shair there's plenty o' room."

"Bless my sowl, where's the plenty o' room?" asked the Captain. "This boat cairries three men and an enchineer, and we're crooded enough in the fo'c'sle."

"Where's that?" she asked, taking all the negotiations out of the hands of her husband, who sat down on the spotted tin box and began to cut tobacco.

"Yonder it is," said Para Handy, indicating the place with a lazy, inelegant, but eloquent gesture of his leg.

"Weel, there's plenty o' room," persisted the woman, – "ye can surely see for yersel' there's plenty o' room; you and your men could sleep at the – at the – the stroup o' the boat there, and ye could mak' us ony kind o' a shake-down doon the stair there" – and she pointed at the hold.

"My coodness! the stroup o' the boat!" exclaimed Para Handy; "you would think it wass a teapot you were taalkin' aboot. And that's no' a doon-stairs at aal, it's the howld. We're no' in the habit of takin' in ludgers in the coastin' tred; I never had wan in the *Fital Spark* in aal my life except the time I cairried Wee Teeny. We havena right accommodation for ludgers; we have no napery, nor enough knives and forks –"

"Onything wad dae for a shove-bye," said the woman. "I'm shair ye wouldna see a dacent man and his wife and twa wee hameless lambs sleepin' in the quarry as lang as ye could gie them a corner to sit doon in on that nice clean boat o' yours."

She was a shrewd woman; her compliment to the *Vital Spark* found the soft side of its captain's nature, and, to the disgust of Macphail the engineer and the annoyance of The Tar – though with the hearty consent of the mate – Jack Flood and his family, with the tin box and the bottle of milk, were ten minutes later installed in the fo'c'sle of the *Vital Spark* as paying guests. The terms arranged were two shillings a night. "You couldna get ludgin's in a good hotel for mich less," said the Captain, and Mrs Flood agreed that that was reasonable.

The crew slept somewhat uncomfortably in the hold, and in the middle watches of the night the Captain wakened at the sound of an infant crying. He sat up, nudged Dougie awake, and moralised.

"Chust listen to that, Dougie," he said, "the wee cratur's greetin' ass naitural ass anything, the same ass if it wass a rale ludgin's or on board wan of them ships that carries passengers to America. It's me that likes to hear it; it's ass homely a thing ass ever happened on this vessel. I wouldna say but maybe it'll be good luck. I'm tellin' you what, Dougie, we'll no' cherge them a d— ha'penny; what do you think, mate?"

"Whatever you say yoursel'," said Dougie.

The wail of the infant continued; they heard Jack Flood get up at the request of his wife and sing. He sang "Rocked in the Cradle of the Deep" – at least he sang two lines of it over and over again, taking liberties with the air that would have much annoyed the original composer if he could have heard him.

"It's chust sublime!" said Para Handy, stretched on a rolled-up sail. "You're a lucky man, Dougie, that iss mairried and has a hoose of your own. Oor two ludgers iss maybe pretty cross when it comes to the quarrelling, but they have no spite at the weans. You would not think that man Flood had the sense to rise up in the muddle of the night and sing 'Rocked in the Cradle of the Deep' at his child. It chust shows you us workin'-men have good he'rts."

"Jeck may have a cood enough he'rt," said Dougie, "but, man! he has a poor, poor ear for music! I wish he would stop it and no' be frightenin' the wean. I'm sure it never did him any herm."

By-and-by the crying and the music ceased, and the only sound to be heard was the snore of The Tar and the lapping of the tide against the run of the vessel.

Sunday was calm and bright, but there was no sign of the lodgers coming on deck till late in the forenoon, much to the surprise of the Captain. At last he heard a loud peremptory whistle from the fo'c'sle, and went forward to see what was wanted. Flood threw up four pairs of boots at him. "Gie them a bit polish," he said airily. "Ye needna be awfu' parteecular," he added, "but they're a' glaur, and we like to be dacent on Sunday."

The Captain, in a daze, lifted the boots and told The Tar to oil them, saying emphatically at the same time to Dougie, "Efter aal, we'll no' let them off with the two shillin's. They're too dirty parteecular."

There was another whistle ten minutes later, and Dougie went to see what was wanted.

"I say, my lad," remarked Mr Flood calmly, "look slippy with the breakfast; we canna sterve here ony langer."

"Are you no' comin' up for't?" asked Dougie in amazement. "It's a fine dry day."

"Dry my auntie!" said Mr Flood. "The wife aye gets her breakfast in her bed on Sundays whether it's wet or dry. Ye'll get the kippered herrin' and the loaf she brung last nicht beside the lum."

The Tar cooked the lodgers' breakfast under protest, saying he was not paid wages for being a saloon steward, and he passed it down to the fo'c'sle.

"Two shilling's a night!" said the Captain. "If I had known what it wass to keep ludgers, it wouldna be two shillin's a night I would be cherging them."

He was even more emphatic on this point when a third whistle came from the fo'c'sle, and

The Tar, on going to see what was wanted now, was informed by Mrs Flood that the cooking was not what she was accustomed to. "I never saw a steamer like this in my life," she said, "first cless, as ye micht say, and no' a table to tak' yer meat aff, and only shelfs to sleep on, and sea-sick nearly the hale nicht to the bargain! Send us doon a pail o' water to clean oor faces."

Para Handy could stand no more. He washed himself carefully, put on his Sunday clothes and his watch-chain, which always gave him great confidence and courage, and went to the fo'c'sle-head. He addressed the lodgers from above.

"Leezy," he said ingratiatingly (for so he had heard Mr Flood designate his wife), " Leezy, you're missing aal the fun doon there; you should come up and see the folk goin' to the church; you never saw such style among the women in aal your days."

"I'll be up in a meenute," she replied quickly; "Jeck, hurry up and hook this."

On the whole, the lodgers and the crew of the *Vital Spark* spent a fairly pleasant Sunday. When the Flood family was not ashore walking in the neighbourhood, it was lying about the deck eating dulse and picking whelks culled from the shore by Jack. The mother kindly supplied the infant with as much dulse and shell-fish as it wanted, and it had for these a most insatiable appetite.

"You shouldna eat any wulks or things of that sort when there's no 'r's' in the month," Para Handy advised her. "They're no' very wholesome then."

"Fiddlesticks!" said Mrs Flood. "I've ett wulks every Fair since I was a wee lassie, and look at me noo! Besides, there's an 'r' in Fair, that puts it a' richt."

That night the infant wailed from the moment they went to bed till it was time to rise in the morning; Jack Flood sang "Rocked in the Cradle of the Deep" till he was hoarse, and the crew in the hold got up next morning very sorry for themselves.

"You'll be takin' the early steamer?" said Para Handy at the first opportunity.

"Och! we're gettin' on fine," said Jack cheerfully; "Leezy and me thinks we'll just put in the week wi' ye," and the wife indicated her hearty concurrence.

"You canna stay here," said the Captain firmly.

"Weel, we're no' goin' to leave, onywye," said Mr Flood, lighting his clay pipe. "We took the ludgin's, and though they're no' as nice as we would like, we're wullin' to put up with them, and ye canna put us oot withoot a week's warnin'."

"My Chove! do you say that?" said Para Handy in amazement. "You're the first and last ludger I'll have on this vessel!"

"A week's notice; it's the law o' the land," said the admirable Mr Flood, "isn't that so, Leezy?"

"Everybody that has sense kens that that's richt," said Mrs Flood. And the Flood family retired *en masse* to the fo'c'sle.

Ten minutes later the *Vital Spark* was getting up steam, and soon there were signs of her immediate departure from the quay.

"Whaur are ye gaun?" cried Jack, coming hurriedly on deck.

"Outward bound," said Para Handy with indifference. "That's a sailor's life for you, here the day and away yesterday."

"To Gleska?" said Mr Flood hopefully.

"Gleska!" said Para Handy. "We'll no' see it for ten months; we're bound for the Rio Grande."

"Whaur's that in a' the warld?" asked Mrs Flood, who had joined her husband on deck.

"Oh! chust in foreign perts," said Para Handy. "Away past the Bay of Biscay, and the first place on your left-hand side after you pass New Zealand. It's where the beasts for the Zoo comes from."

In four minutes the Flood family were off the ship, and struggling up the quay with the spotted tin trunk, and the *Vital Spark* was starting for Bowling.

"I'm a stupid man," said Para Handy in a few minutes after leaving the quay. "Here we're away and forgot aal aboot the money for the ludgin's."

9

A LOST MAN

IT was a dirty evening, coming on to dusk, and the *Vital Spark* went walloping drunkenly down Loch Fyne with a cargo of oak bark, badly trimmed. She staggered to every shock of the sea; the waves came combing over her quarter, and Dougie the mate began to wish they had never sailed that day from Kilcatrine. They had struggled round the point of Pennymore, the prospect looking every moment blacker, and he turned a dozen projects over in his mind for inducing Para Handy to anchor somewhere till the morning. At last he remembered Para's partiality for anything in the way of long-shore gaiety, and the lights of the village of Furnace gave him an idea.

"Ach! man, Peter," said he, "did we no' go away and forget this wass the night of the baal at Furnace? What do you say to going in and joining the spree?"

"You're feared, Dougie," said the Captain; "you're scared to daith for your life, in case you'll have to die and leave your money. You're thinkin' you'll be drooned, and that's the way you want to put her into Furnace. Man! but you're tumid, tumid! Chust look at me – no' the least put aboot. That's becaause I'm a Macfarlane, and a Macfarlane never was bate yet, never in this world! I'm no' goin' to stop the night for any baal – we must be in Clyde on Friday; besides, we havena the clothes wi' us for a baal. Forbye, who'll buy the tickets? Eh? Tell me that! Who'll buy the tickets?"

"Ach! you don't need tickets for a Furnace baal," said Dougie, flicking the spray from his ear,

and looking longingly at the village they were nearing. "You don't need tickets for a Furnace baal as long as you ken the man at the door and taalk the Gaalic at him. And your clothes'll do fine if you oil your boots and put on a kind of a collar. What's the hurry for Clyde? It'll no' run dry. In weather like this, too! It's chust a temptin' of Providence. I had a dream yonder last night that wasna canny. Chust a temptin' of Providence."

"I wudna say but it is," agreed the Captain weakly, putting the vessel a little to starboard; "it's many a day since I was at a spree in Furnace. Are you sure the baal's the night?"

"Of course I am," said Dougie emphatically; "it only started yesterday."

"Weel, if you're that keen on't, we'll maybe be chust as weel to put her in till the mornin'," said Para Handy, steering hard for Furnace Bay; and in a little he knocked down to the engines with the usual, "Stop her, Macphail, when you're ready."

All the crew of the *Vital Spark* went to the ball, but they did not dance much, though it was the boast of Para Handy that he was "a fine strong dancer". The last to come down to the vessel in the morning when the ball stopped, because the paraffin-oil was done, was the Captain, walking on his heels, with his pea-jacket tightly buttoned on his chest, and his round, go-ashore pot hat, as he used to say himself, "on three hairs". It was a sign that he felt intensely satisfied with everything.

"I'm feeling chust sublime," he said to Dougie, smacking his lips and thumping himself on the chest as he took his place at the wheel, and the *Vital Spark* resumed her voyage down the loch. "I am chust like the eagle that knew the youth in the Scruptures. It's a fine, fine thing a spree, though I wass not in the trum for dancing. I met sixteen cousins yonder, and them all in the committee. They were the proud men last night to be having a captain for a cousin, and them only quarry-men. It's the educaation, Dougie; educaation gives you the nerve, and if you have the nerve you can go round the world."

"You werena very far roond the world, whatever o't," unkindly interjected the engineer, who stuck up his head at the moment.

The Captain made a push at him angrily with his foot. "Go down, Macphail," he said, "and do not be making a display of your ignorance on this ship. Stop you till I get you at Bowling! Not round the world! Man, I wass twice at Ullapool, and took the *Fital Spark* to Ireland wance, without a light on her. There iss not a port I am not acquent with from the Tail of the Bank to Cairndow, where they keep the two New Years. And Campbeltown, ay, or Barra, or Tobermory. I'm telling you when I am in them places it's Captain Peter Macfarlane iss the mich-respected man. If you were a rale enchineer and not chust a fireman, I would be asking you to my ludgings to let you see the things I brought from my voyages."

The engineer drew in his head and resumed the perusal of a penny novelette.

"He thinks I'm frightened for him," said the Captain, winking darkly to his mate. "It iss because I am too cuvil to him: if he angers me, I'll show him. It is chust spoiling the boat having a man like that in cherge of her enchines, and her such a fine smert boat, with me, and a man like me, in command of her."

"And there's mysel', too, the mate," said Dougie; "I'm no' bad mysel'."

Below Minard rocks the weather grew worse again: the same old seas smashed over the *Vital Spark*. "She's pitching aboot chust like a washin'-boyne," said Dougie apprehensively. "That's the worst of them oak-bark cargoes."

"Like a washin'-boyne!" cried Para Handy indignantly; "she's chust doing sublime. I wass in boats in my time where you would need to be bailing the watter out of your top-boots every here and there. The smertest boat in the tred; stop you till I have a pound of my own, and I will paint her till you'll take her for a yat if it wasna for the lum. You and your washin'-boyne! A washin'-boyne wudna do you any herm, my laad, and that's telling you."

They were passing Lochgair; the steamer *Cygnet* overtook and passed them as if they had been standing, somebody shouting to them from her deck.

Para Handy refrained from looking. It always annoyed him to be passed this way by other craft; and in summer time, when the turbine *King Edward* or the *Lord of the Isles* went past him like a streak of lightning, he always retired below to hide his feelings. He did not look at the *Cygnet*. "Ay, ay," he said to Dougie, "if I was telling Mr Macbrayne the umpudence of them fellows, he would put a stop to it in a meenute, but I will not lose them their chobs; poor sowls! maybe they have wifes and families. That'll be Chonny Mactavish takin' his fun of me; you would think he wass a wean. Chust like them brats of boys that come to the riverside when we'll be going up the Clyde at Yoker and cry, 'Columbia, ahoy!' at us – the duvvle's own!"

As the Cygnet disappeared in the distance, with a figure waving at her stern, a huge sea struck the Vital Spark and swept her from stem to stern, almost washing the mate, who was hanging on to a stay, overboard.

"Tar! Tar!" cried the Captain. "Go and get a ha'ad o' that bucket or it'll be over the side."

There was no response. The Tar was not visible, and a wild dread took possession of Para Handy.

"Let us pause and consider," said he to himself; "was The Tar on board when we left Furnace?"

They searched the vessel high and low for the missing member of the crew, who was sometimes given to fall asleep in the fo'c'sle at the time he was most needed. But there was no sign of him. "I ken fine he wass on board when we started," said the Captain, distracted, "for I heard him sputtin'. Look again, Dougie, like a good laad." Dougie looked again, for he, too, was sure The Tar had returned from the ball with him. "I saw him with my own eyes," he said, "two of him, the same as if he was a twins; that iss the curse of drink in a place like Furance." But the search was in vain, even though the engineer said he had seen The Tar an hour ago.

"Weel, there's a good man gone!" said Para Handy. "Och! poor Tar! It was yon last smasher of a sea. He's over the side. Poor laad! poor laad! Cot bless me, dyin' without a word of Gaalic in his mooth! It's a chudgment on us for the way we were carryin' on, chust a chudgment; not another drop of drink will I drink, except maybe beer. Or at a New Year time. I'm blaming you, Dougie, for making us stop at Furnace for a baal I wudna give a snuff for. You are chust a disgrace to the vessel, with your smokin' and your drinkin', and your ignorance. It iss time you were livin' a better life for the sake of your wife and femily. If it wass not for you makin' me go into Furnace last night, The Tar would be to the fore yet, and I would not need to be sending a telegram to his folk from Ardrishaig. If I wass not steering the boat, I would break my he'rt greetin' for the poor laad that never did anybody any herm. Get oot the flag from below my bunk, give it a syne in the pail, and put it at half-mast, and we'll go into Ardrishaig and send a telegram – it'll be a sixpence. It'll be a telegram with a sore he'rt, I'll assure you. I do not know what I will say in it, Dougie. It will not do to break it too much to them; maybe we will send the two telegrams – that'll be a shilling. We'll say in the first wan – 'Your son, Colin, left the boat to-day': and in the next wan we will say – 'He iss not coming back, he iss drooned.' Och! och! poor Tar, amn't I sorry for him? I was chust going to put up his wages a shillin' on Setturday."

The *Vital Spark* went in close to Ardrishaig pier just as the *Cygnet* was leaving after taking in a cargo of herring-boxes. Para Handy and Dougie went ashore in the punt, the Captain with his hands washed and his watch-chain on as a tribute of respect for the deceased. Before they could send off the telegram it was necessary that they should brace themselves for the melancholy occasion. "No drinking, chust wan gless of beer," said Para Handy, and they entered a discreet contiguous public-house for this purpose.

The Tar himself was standing at the counter having a refreshment, with one eye wrapped up in a handkerchief.

"Dalmighty!" cried the Captain, staggered at the sight, and turning pale. "What are you doing here with your eye in a sling?"

"What's your business?" retorted The Tar coolly. "I'm no' in your employ anyway."

"What way that?" asked Para Handy sharply.

"Did you no' give me this black eye and the sack last night at the baal, and tell me I wass never to set foot on the *Vital Spark* again? It was gey mean o' you to go away withoot lettin' me get my dunnage oot, and that's the way I came here with the *Cygnet* to meet you. Did you no' hear me roarin' on you when we passed?"

"Weel done! weel done!" said Para Handy soothingly, with a wink at his mate. "But ach! I wass only in fun, Colin; it wass a jeenk; it wass chust a baur aalthegither. Come away back to the boat like a smert laad. I have a shilling here I wass going to spend anyway. Colin, what'll you take? We thought you were over the side and drooned, and you are here, quite dry as usual."

10

HURRICANE JACK

I VERY often hear my friend the Captain speak of Hurricane Jack in terms of admiration and devotion, which would suggest that Jack is a sort of demigod. The Captain always refers to Hurricane Jack as the most experienced seaman of modern times, as the most fearless soul that ever wore oilskins, the handsomest man in Britain, so free with his money he would fling it at the birds, so generally accomplished that it would be a treat to be left a month on a desert island alone with him.

"Why is he called Hurricane Jack?" I asked the Captain once.

"What the duvvle else would you caal him?" asked Para Handy. "Nobody ever caals him anything else than Hurricane Jeck."

 "Quite so, but why?" I persisted.

Para Handy scratched the back of his neck, made the usual gesture as if he were going to scratch his ear, and then cheeked himself in the usual way to survey his hand as if it were a beautiful example of Greek sculpture. His hand, I may say, is almost as large as a Belfast ham.

"What way wass he called Hurricane Jeck?" said he. "Well, I'll soon tell you that. He wass not always known by that name; that wass a name he got for the time he stole the sheep."

"Stole the sheep!" I said, a little bewildered, for I failed to see how an incident of that kind would give rise to such a name.

"Yes; what you might call stole," said Para Handy hastily; "but, och! it wass only wan smaal wee sheep he lifted on a man that never went to the church, and chust let him take it! Hurricane Jeck would not steal a fly – no, nor two flies, from a Chrustian; he's the perfect chentleman in that."

"Tell me all about it," I said.

"I'll soon do that," said he, putting out his hand to admire it again, and in doing so upsetting his glass. "Tut, tut!" he said. "Look what I have done – knocked doon my gless; it wass a good thing there wass nothing in it.

"Hurricane Jeck," said the Captain, when I had taken the hint and put something in it, "iss a man that can sail anything and go anywhere, and aalways be the perfect chentleman. A millionaire's yat or a washin'-boyne – it's aal the same to Jeck; he would sail the wan chust as smert as the other, and land on the quay as spruce ass if he wass newly come from a baal. Oh, man! the cut of his jeckets! And never anything else but 'lastic-sided boots, even in the coorsest weather! If you would see him, you would see a man that's chust sublime, and that careful about his 'lastic-sided boots he would never stand at the wheel unless there wass a bass below his feet. He'll aye be oil-oiling at his hair, and buying hard hats for going ashore with: I never saw a man wi' a finer heid for the hat, and in some of the vessels he wass in he would have the full of a bunker of hats. Hurricane Jeck wass brought up in the China clupper tred, only he wassna called Hurricane Jeck then, for he hadna stole the sheep till efter that. He wass captain of the *Dora Young*, wan of them cluppers; he's a hand on a gaabert the now, but aalways the perfect chentleman."

"It seems a sad downcome for a man to be a gabbart hand after having commanded a China clipper," I ventured to remark. "What was the reason of his change?"

"Bad luck," said Para Handy. "Chust bad luck. The fellow never got fair-play. He would aye be somewhere takin' a gless of something wi' somebody, for he's a fine big cheery chap. I mind splendid when he wass captain on the clupper, he had a fine hoose of three rooms and a big decanter, wi' hot and cold watter, oot at Pollokshaws. When you went oot to the hoose to see Hurricane Jeck in them days, time slupped bye. But he wassna known as Hurricane Jeck then, for it wass before he stole the sheep."

"You were just going to tell me something about that," I said.

"Jeck iss wan man in a hundred, and ass good ass two if there wass anything in the way of trouble, for, man! he's strong, strong! He has a back on him like a shipping-box, and when he will come down Tarbert quay on a Friday night after a good fishing, and the trawlers are arguing, it's two yerds to the step with him and a bash in the side of his hat for fair defiance.But he never hit a man twice, for he's aye the perfect chentleman iss Hurricane Jeck. Of course, you must understand, he wass not known as Hurricane Jeck till the time I'm going to tell you of, when he stole the sheep.

"I have not trevelled far mysel' yet, except Ullapool and the time I wass at Ireland; but Hurricane Jeck in his time has been at every place on the map, and some that's no'. Chust wan of Brutain's hardy sons – that's what he iss. As weel kent in Calcutta as if he wass in the Coocaddens, and he could taalk a dozen of their foreign kinds of languages if he cared to take the bother. When he would be leaving a port, there wassna a leddy in the place but what would be doon on the quay wi' her Sunday clothes on and a bunch o' floo'ers for his cabin. And when he would be sayin' good-bye to them from the brudge, he would chust take off his hat and give it a shoogle, and put it on again; his manners wass complete. The first thing he would do when he reached any place wass to go ashore and get his boots brushed, and then sing 'Rule Britannia' roond aboot the docks. It wass a sure way to get freend or foe aboot you, he said, and he wass aye as ready for the wan as for the other. Brutain's hardy son!

"He made the fastest passages in his time that wags ever made in the tea trade, and still and on he would meet you like a common working-man. There wass no pride or nonsense of that sort aboot Hurricane Jeck; but, mind you, though I'm callin' him Hurricane Jeck, he wasna Hurricane Jeck till the time he stole the sheep."

"I don't like to press you, Captain, but I'm anxious to hear about that sheep," I said patiently.

"I'm comin' to't," said Para Handy. "Jeck had the duvvle's own bad luck; he couldna take a gless by-ordinar' but the ship went wrong on him, and he lost wan job efter the other, but he wass never anything else but the perfect chentleman. When he had not a penny in his pocket, he would

borrow a shilling from you, and buy you a stick pipe for yourself chust for good nature –"

"A stick pipe?" I repeated interrogatively.

"Chust a stick pipe – or a wudden pipe, or whatever you like to call it. He had three medals and a clock that wouldna go for saving life at sea, but that wass before he wass Hurricane Jeck, mind you; for at that time he hadna stole the sheep."

"I'm dying to hear about that sheep," I said.

"I'll soon tell you about the sheep," said Para Handy. "It wass a thing that happened when him and me wass sailing on the *Elizabeth Ann*, a boat that belonged to Girvan, and a smert wan too, if she wass in any kind of trum at aal. We would be going here and there aboot the West Coast with wan thing and another, and not costing the owners mich for coals if coals wass our cargo. It wass wan Sunday we were passing Caticol in Arran, and in a place yonder where there wass not a hoose in sight we saw a herd of sheep eating gress near the shore. As luck would have it, there wass not a bit of butcher-meat on board the *Elizabeth Ann* for the Sunday dinner, and Jeck cocked his eye at the sheep and says to me, 'Yonder's some sheep lost, poor things; what do you say to taking the punt and going ashore to see if there's anybody's address on them?'

" 'Whatever you say yoursel',' I said to Jeck, and we stopped the vessel and went ashore, the two of us, and looked the sheep high and low, but there wass no address on them. 'They're lost, sure enough,' said Jeck, pulling some heather and putting it in his pocket – he wassna Hurricane Jeck then – 'they're lost, sure enough, Peter. Here's a nice wee wan nobody would ever miss, chust the very thing for a coal vessel,' and before you could say 'knife' he had it killed and carried to the punt. Oh, he iss a smert, smert fellow with his hands; he could do anything.

"We rowed ass caalm ass we could oot to the vessel, and we had chust got the deid sheep on board when we heard a roarin' and whustling.

" 'Taalk about Arran being releegious!' said Jeck. 'Who's that whustling on the Lord's day?'

"The man that wass whustling wass away up on the hill, and we could see him coming running doon the hill the same ass if he would break every leg he had on him.

" 'I'll bate you he'll say it's his sheep,' said Jeck. 'Weel, we'll chust anchor the vessel here till we hear what he hass to say, for if we go away and never mind the cratur he'll find oot somewhere else it's the *Elizabeth Ann*.'

"When the fermer and two shepherds came oot to the *Elizabeth Ann* in a boat, she wass lying at anchor, and we were all on deck, every man wi' a piece o' heather in his jecket.

" 'I saw you stealing my sheep,' said the fermer, coming on deck, furious. 'I'll have every man of you jiled for this.'

" 'Iss the man oot of his wuts?' said Jeck. 'Drink – chust drink! Nothing else but drink! If you were a sober Christian man, you would be in the church at this 'oor in Arran, and not oot on the hill recovering from last night's carry-on in Loch Ranza, and imagining you are seeing things that's not there at aal, at aal.'

" 'I saw you with my own eyes steal the sheep and take it on board,' said the fermer, nearly choking with rage.

" 'What you saw was my freend and me gathering a puckle heather for oor jeckets,' said Jeck, 'and if ye don't believe me you can search the ship from stem to stern.'

" 'I'll soon do that,' said the fermer, and him and his shepherds went over every bit of the *Elizabeth Ann*. They never missed a corner you could hide a moose in, but there wass no sheep nor sign of sheep anywhere.

" 'Look at that, Macalpine,' said Jeck. 'I have a good mind to have you up for inflammation of character. But what could you expect from a man that would be whustling on the hill like a peesweep on a Sabbath when he should be in the church. It iss a good thing for you, Macalpine, it iss a Sabbath, and I can keep my temper.'

" 'I could swear I saw you lift the sheep,' said the fermer, quite vexed.

" 'Saw your auntie! Drink; nothing but the cursed drink!' said Jeck, and the fermer and his shepherds went away with their tails behind their legs.

"We lay at anchor till it was getting dark, and then we lifted the anchor and took off the sheep that wass tied to it when we put it oot. 'It's a good thing salt mutton,' said Hurricane Jeck as we sailed away from Caticol, and efter that the name he always got wass Hurricane Jeck."

"But why 'Hurricane Jeck'?" I asked, more bewildered than ever.

"Holy smoke! am I no' tellin' ye?" said Para Handy. "It wass beeause he stole the sheep."

But I don't understand it yet.

11

PARA HANDY'S APPRENTICE

THE owner of the *Vital Spark* one day sent for her Captain, who oiled his hair, washed himself with hot water and a scrubbing-brush, got The Tar to put three coats of blacking on his boots, attired himself in his good clothes, and went up to the office in a state of some anxiety. "It's either a rise in pay," he said to himself, "or he's heard aboot the night we had in Campbeltown. That's the worst of high jeenks; they're aye stottin' back and hittin' you on the nose; if it's no' a sore heid, you've lost a pound-note, and if it's nothing you lost, it's somebody clypin' on you." But when he got to the office and was shown into the owner's room, he was agreeably enough surprised to find that though there was at first no talk about a rise of pay, there was, on the other hand, no complaint.

"What I wanted to see you about, Peter," said the owner, "is my oldest boy Alick. He's tired of school and wants to go to sea."

"Does he, does he? Poor fellow!" said Para Handy. "Och, he's but young yet, he'll maybe get better. Hoo's the mustress keepin'?"

"She's very well, thank you, Peter," said the owner. "But I'm anxious about that boy of mine. I feel sure that he'll run away some day on a ship; he's just the very sort to do it and I want you to help me. I'm going to send him one trip with you, and I want you to see that he's put off the notion of being a sailor – you understand? I don't care what you do to him so long as you don't break a leg on him, or let him fall over the side. Give him it stiff."

"Chust that!" said the Captain. "Iss he a boy that reads novelles?"

"Fair daft for them!" said the owner. "That's the cause of the whole thing."

"Then I think I can cure him in wan trip, and it'll no' hurt him either."

"I'll send him down to the *Vital Spark* on Wednesday, just before you start," said the owner. "And, by the way, if you manage to sicken him of the idea, I wouldn't say but there might be a small increase in your wages."

"Och, there's no occasion for that," said Para Handy.

On the Wednesday a boy about twelve years of age, with an Eton suit and a Saturday-to-Monday hand-bag, came down to the wharf in a cab alone, opened the door of the cab hurriedly, and almost fell into the arms of Para Handy, who was on shore to meet him.

"Are you the apprentice for the *Fital Spark*?" asked the Captain affably. "Your name'll be Alick?"

"Yes," said the boy. "Are you the Captain?"

"That's me," said the Captain. "Gie me a haad o' your portmanta," and taking it out of Alick's hand, he led the way to the side of the wharf, where the *Vital Spark* was lying, with a cargo of coals that left her very little free-board, and all her crew on deck awaiting developments. "I'm sorry," he said, "we havena any gangway, but I'll hand you doon to Dougie, and you'll be aal right if your gallowses'll no' give way."

"What! is THAT the boat I'm to go on?" cried the boy, astounded.

"Yes," said the Captain, with a little natural irritation. "And what's wrong with her? The smertest boat in the tred. Stop you till you see her goin' roond Ardlamont!"

"But she's only a coal boat; she's very wee," said Alick. "I never thought my father would apprentice me on a boat like that."

"But it's aye a beginnin'," explained the Captain, with remarkable patience. "You must aye start sailorin' some way, and there's many a man on the brudge of Atlantic liners the day that began on boats no bigger than the *Fital Spark*. If you don't believe me, Dougie'll tell you himsel'. Here, Dougie, catch a haad o' oor new apprentice, and watch you don't dirty his clean collar wi' your hands." So saying, he slung Alick down to the mate, and ten minutes later the *Vital Spark,* with her new apprentice on board, was coughing her asthmatic way down the river outward bound for Tarbert. The boy watched the receding wharf with mixed feelings.

"What do you say to something to eat?" asked the Captain, as soon as his command was under way. "I'll tell The Tar to boil you an egg, and you'll have a cup of tea. You're a fine high-spurited boy, and a growin' boy needs aal the meat he can get. Watch that rope; see and no' dirty your collar; it would never do to see an apprentice wi' a dirty collar."

Alick took the tea and the boiled egg, and thought regretfully that life at sea, so far, was proving very different from what he had expected.

"Where are we bound for?" he asked.

"Oh! a good long trup," said the Captain. "As far as Tarbert and back again. You'll be an A.B. by the time you come back."

"And will I get wearing brass buttons?" inquired Alick.

"Brass buttons!" exclaimed Para Handy. "Man, they're oot o' date at sea aalthegither; it's nothing but hooks and eyes, and far less trouble to keep them clean."

"Can I start learning to climb the mast now?" asked Alick, who was naturally impatient to acquire the elements of his new profession.

"Climb the mast!" cried Para Handy, horrified. "There wass never an apprentice did that on my vessel, and never will; it would dirty aal your hands! I see a shoo'er o' rain comin'; there's nothing worse for the young sailor than gettin' damp; away doon below like a good boy, and rest you, and I'll give you a roar when the rain's past."

Alick went below bewildered. In all the books he had read there had been nothing to prepare him for such coddling on a first trip to sea; so far, there was less romance about the business than he could have found at home in Athole Gardens. It rained all afternoon, and he was not permitted on deck; jelly "pieces" were sent down to him at intervals. The Tar was continually boiling him eggs; he vaguely felt some dreadful indignity in eating them, but his appetite compelled him, and the climax of the most hum-drum day he had ever spent came at night when the Captain insisted

on his taking gruel to keep off the cold, and on his fastening his stocking round his neck.

Alick was wakened next morning by The Tar standing at the side of his bunk with tea on a tray.

"Apprentices aye get their breakfast in their bed," said The Tar, who had been carefully coached by the Captain what he was to do. "Sit up and take this, and then have a nice sleep to yoursel', for it's like to be rainin' aal day, and you canna get on deck."

"Surely I can't melt," said the boy, exasperated. "I'll not learn much seamanship lying here."

"You would maybe get your daith o' cold," said The Tar, "and a nice-like job we would have nursin' you." He turned to go on deck when an idea that Para Handy had not given him came into his head, and with great solemnity he said to the boy, "Perhaps you would like to see a newspaper; we could put ashore and buy wan for you to keep you from wearyin'."

"I wouldn't object to 'Comic Cuts'," said Alick, finding the whole illusion of life on the deep slipping from him.

But "Comic Cuts" did not come down. Instead, there came the Captain with a frightful and familiar thing – the strapful of school-books to escape from which Alick had first proposed a sailor's life. Para Handy had sent to Athole Gardens for them the previous day.

"Shipmate ahoy!" he cried, cheerily stumping down to the fo'c'sle. "You'll be frightened you left your books behind, but I sent The Tar for them, and here they are," and, unbuckling the strap, he poured the unwelcome volumes on the apprentice's lap.

"Who ever heard of an apprentice sailor taking his school-books to sea with him?" said Alick, greatly disgusted.

"Who ever heard o' anything else?" retorted the Captain. "Do you think a sailor doesna need any educaation? Every apprentice has to keep going at his Latin and Greek, and Bills of Parcels, and the height of Ben Nevis, and Grammar, and aal the rest of it. That's what they call navigation, and if you havena the navigation, where are you? Chust that, where are you?"

"Do you meant to tell me that when you were an apprentice you learned Latin and Greek, and all the rest of that rot?" asked Alick, amazed.

"Of course I did," said the Captain unblushingly. "Every day till my heid wass sore!"

"Nature Knowledge, too?" asked Alick.

"Nature Knowledge!" cried Para Handy. "At Nature Knowledge I wass chust sublime! I could do it with my eyes shut. Chust you take your books, Alick, like a sailor, and wire into your navigation, and it'll be the brudge for you aal the sooner."

There were several days of this unromantic life for the boy, who had confidently expected to find the career of a sea apprentice something very different. He had to wash and dress himself every morning as scrupulously as ever he did at home for Kelvinside Academy; Para Handy said that was a thing that was always expected from apprentices, and he even went further and sent Alick back to the water-bucket on the ground that his neck and ears required a little more attention. A certain number of hours each day, at least, were ostensibly devoted to the study of "Navigation", which, the boy was disgusted to find, was only another name for the lessons he had had at the Academy. He was not allowed on deck when it was wet without an umbrella, which the Captain had unearthed from somewhere; it was in vain he rebelled against breakfast in bed, gruel, and jelly "pieces".

"If this is being a sailor, I would sooner be in a Sunday School," said Alick finally.

"Ooh! you're doin' splendid," said Para Handy. "A fine high-spurited laad! We'll make a sailor of you by the time we're back at Bowling if you keep your health. It's pretty cold the night; away doon to your bunk like a smert laad, and The Tar'll take doon a hot-watter bottle for your feet in a meenute or two."

When the *Vital Spark* got back to the Clyde, she was not three minutes at the wharf when her apprentice deserted her.

Para Handy went up to the owner's office in the afternoon with the boy's school-books and the Saturday-to-Monday bag.

"I don't know how you managed it," said Alick's father, quite pleased; "but he's back yonder this morning saying a sailor's life's a fraud, and that he wouldn't be a sailor for any money. And by the fatness of him, I should say you fed him pretty well."

"Chust that!" said Para Handy. "The Tar would be aye boilin' an egg for him noo and then.

Advice to a boy iss not much use; the only thing for it iss kindness, chust kindness. If I wass wantin' to keep that boy at the sailin', I would have taken the rope's-end to him, and he would be a sailor chust to spite me. There wass some taalk aboot a small rise in the pay, but och –"

"That's all right, Peter; I've told the cashier," said the owner, and the Captain of the *Vital Spark* went down the stair beaming.

12

QUEER CARGOES

"THE worst cargo ever I sailed wi'," said Macphail the engineer, "was a wheen o' thae Mahommedan pilgrims: it wasna Eau de Colong they had on their hankies."

"Mahommedans!" said Para Handy, with his usual suspicions of the engineer's foreign experience – "Mahommedans! Where were they bound for? Was't Kirkintilloch?"

"Kirkintilloch's no' in Mahommeda," said Macphail nastily. "I'm talkin' aboot rale sailin', no' wyding in dubs, the way some folk does a' their days."

"Chust that! chust that!" retorted the Captain, sniffing. "I thought it wass maybe on the Port Dundas Canal ye had them."

"There was ten or eleeven o' them died every nicht," proceeded Macphail, contemptuous of these interruptions. "We just gied them the heave over the side, and then full speed aheid to make up for the seven meenutes."

"Like enough you would ripe their pockets first," chimed in Dougie. "The worst cargo ever I sailed with wass leemonade bottles; you could hear them clinking aal night, and not wan drop of stumulents on board! It wass duvvelish vexing."

"The worst cargo ever I set eyes on," ventured The Tar timidly, in presence of these hardened mariners, "wass sawdust for stuffing dolls."

"Sawdust would suit you fine, Colin," said the Captain. "I'll warrant you got plenty of sleep that trup.

"You're there and you're taalking about cargoes," proceeded Para Handy, "but there's not wan of you had the experience I had, and that wass with a cargo of shows for Tarbert Fair. They were to go with a luggage-steamer, but the luggage-steamer met with a kind of an accident, and wass late of getting to the Broomielaw: she twisted wan of her port-holes or something like that, and we got the chob. It's me that wassna wantin' it, for it wass no credit to a smert boat like the *Fital Spark*, but you ken yoursel' what owners iss; they would carry coal tar made up in delf crates if they get the freight for it."

"I wouldna say but what you're right," remarked Dougie agreeably.

"A stevedore would go wrong in the mind if he saw the hold of the vessel efter them showmen got their stuff on board. You would think it wass a pawnshop struck wi' a sheet o' lightning. There wass everything ever you saw at a show except the coconuts and the comic polisman. We started at three o'clock in the mornin', and a lot of the show people made a bargain to come wi' us to look efter their stuff. There wass the Fattest Woman in the World, No-Boned Billy or the Boy Serpent, the Mesmerising Man, another man very namely among the Crowned Heads for walkin' on stilts, and the heid man o' the shows, a chap they called Mr Archer. At the last meenute they put on a wee piebald pony that could pick oot any card you asked from a pack. If you don't believe me, Macphail, there's Dougie; you can ask him yoursel'."

"You're quite right, Peter," said Dougie emphatically. "I'll never forget it. What are you goin' to tell them aboot the Fair?" he added suspiciously.

"It's a terrible life them show folk has!" resumed the Captain, without heeding the question. "Only English people would put up with it; poor craturs, I wass sorry for them! Fancy them goin' aboot from place to place aal the year roond, wi' no homes! I would a hundred times sooner be a sailor the way I am. But they were nice enough to us, and we got on fine, and before you could say 'knife' Dougie wass flirtin' wi' the Fattest Woman in the World."

"Don't believe him, boys," said the mate, greatly embarrassed. "I never even kent her Chrustian name."

"When we got the shows discherged at Tarbert, Mr Archer came and presented us aal with a free pass for everything except the stilts. 'You'll no' need to put on your dress clothes,' says he. He wass a cheery wee chap, though he wass chust an Englishman. Dougie and me went ashore and had a royal night of it. I don't know if ever you wass at a Tarbert Fair, Macphail – you were aye that busy learnin' the names of the foreign places you say you traivelled to, that you wouldn't have the time; but I'll warrant you it's worth while seein'. There's things to be seen there you couldna see the like of in London. Dougie made for the tent of the mesmeriser and the Fattest Woman in the World whenever we got there: he thought she would maybe be dancin' or something of that sort, but aal she did was to sit on a chair and look fat. There wass a crood roond her nippin' her to make sure she wasna padded, and when we got in she cried, 'Here's my intended man, Mr Dugald; stand aside and let him to the front to see his bonny wee rosebud. Dugald, darling, you see I'm true to you and wearin' your ring yet,' and she showed the crood a brass ring you could tie boats to."

"She wass a caaution!" said Dougie. "But what's the use of rakin' up them old stories?"

"Then we went to the place where No-Boned Billy or the Boy Serpent wass tying himself in knots and jumpin' through girrs. It was truly sublime! It bates me to know hoo they do it, but I suppose it's chust educaation."

"It's nothing else," said the mate. "Educaation'll do anything for you if you take it when you're young, and have the money as weel."

"Every noo and then we would be takin' a gless of yon red lemonade they sell at aal the Fairs, till Dougie got dizzy and had to go to a public-house for beer."

"Don't say a word aboot yon," interrupted the mate anxiously.

"It's aal right, Dougie, we're among oorsel's. Weel, as I wass sayin', when he got the beer, Dougie, right or wrong, wass for goin' to see the fortune-teller. She wass an Italian-lookin' body that did the spaein', and for a sixpence she gave Dougie the finest fortune ever you heard of. He wass to be left a lot of money when he wass fifty-two, and mairry the dochter of a landed chentleman. But he wass to watch a man wi' curly hair that would cross his path, and he wass to mind and never go a voyage abroad in the month o' September. Dougie came out of the Italian

spaewife's in fine trum wi' himsel', and nothing would do him but another vusit to the Fattest Woman in the World."

"Noo, chust you be canny what you're at next!" again broke in the mate. "You said you would never tell anybody."

"Who's tellin' anybody?" asked Para Handy impatiently. "I'm only mentionin' it to Macphail and Colin here. The mesmeriser wass readin' bumps when we got into the tent, and Dougie wass that full o' the fine fortune the Italian promised him that he must be up to have his bumps read. The mesmeriser felt aal the bumps on Dougie's heid, no' forgettin' the wan he got on the old New Year at Cairndow, and he said it wass wan of the sublimest heids he ever passed under his hands. 'You are a sailor,' he said to Dougie, 'but acoordin' to your bumps you should have been a munister. You had a fine, fine heid for waggin'. There's great strength of will behind the ears, and the back of the foreheid's packed wi' animosity.'

"When the readin' of the bumps wass done, and Dougie wass nearly greetin' because his mother didna send him to the College in time, the mesmeriser said he would put him in a trance, and then he would see fine fun."

"Stop it, Peter," protested the mate. "If you tell them, I'll never speak to you again."

Para Handy paid no attention, but went on with his narrative. "He got Dougie to stare him in the eye the time he wass working his hands like anything, and Dougie was in a trance in five meenutes. Then the man made him think he wass a railway train, and Dougie went on his hands and knees up and doon the pletform whustlin' for tunnels. Efter that he made him think he wass a singer – and a plank of wud – and a soger – and a hen. I wass black affronted to see the mate of the *Fital Spark* a hen. But the best of the baur was when he took the Fattest Woman in the World up on the pletform and mairried her to Dougie in front of the whole of Tarbert."

"You gave me your word you would never mention it," interrupted the mate, perspiring with annoyance.

"Then the mesmeriser made Dougie promise he would come back at twelve o'clock the next day and take his new wife on the honeymoon. When Dougie wass wakened oot of the trance, he didn't mind onything aboot it."

"Neither I did," said the mate.

"Next day, at ten meenutes to twelve, when we were makin' ready to start for the Clyde, my mate here took a kind of a tirrivee, and wass for the shows again. I saw the dregs of the mesmerisin' wass on the poor laad, so I took him and gave him a gill of whisky with sulphur in it, and whipped him on board the boat and off to the Clyde before the trance came on at its worst. It never came back."

"Iss that true?" asked The Tar.

"If Dougie wass here – of course it iss true," said the Captain.

"All I can mind aboot it is the whisky and sulphur," said Dougie. "That's true enough."

13

IN SEARCH OF A WIFE

THE TAR had only got his first week's wages after they were raised a shilling, when the sense of boundless wealth took possession of him, and went to his head like glory. He wondered how on earth he could spend a pound a week. Nineteen shillings were only some loose coins in your pocket, that always fell through as if they were red-hot: a pound-note was different, the pleasure of not changing it till maybe to-morrow was like a wage in itself. He kept the pound-note untouched for three days, and then dreamed one night that he lost it through a hole in his pocket. There were really holes in his pockets, a fact that had never troubled him before; so the idea of getting a wife to mend them flashed on him. He was alarmed at the notion at first – it was so much out of his daily routine of getting up and putting on the fire, and cooking for the crew, and working the winch, and eating and sleeping – so he put it out of his head; but it always came back when he thought of the responsibility of a pound a week, so at last he went up to Para Handy and said to him sheepishly, "I wass thinking to mysel' yonder that maybe it wouldna be a bad plan for me to be takin' a kind of a wife."

"Capital! First-rate! Good for you, Colin!" said the Captain. "A wife's chust the very thing you're needing. Your guernsays iss no credit to the *Fital Spark* – indeed they'll be giving the boat a bad name; and I aalways like to see everything in nice trum aboot her. I would maybe try wan mysel', but I'm that busy on the boat with wan thing and another, me being Captain of her, I havena mich time for keeping a hoose. But och! there's no hurry for me; I am chust nine and two-twenties of years old, no' countin' the year I wass workin' in the sawmull. What wass the gyurl you were thinkin' on?"

"Och, I didna get that length," said The Tar, getting very red in the face at having the business rushed like that.

"Weel, you would need to look slippy," said Para Handy. "There's fellows on shore with white collars on aal the time going aboot picking up the smert wans."

"I wass chust thinkin' maybe you would hear of somebody aboot Loch Fyne that would be suitable: you ken the place better nor me."

"I ken every bit of it," said Para Handy, throwing out his chest. "I wass born aal along this loch-side, and brocht up wi' an auntie. What kind of a wan would you be wantin'?"

"Och, I would chust leave that to yoursel'," said The Tar. "Maybe if she had a puckle money it wouldna be any herm."

"Money!" cried the Captain. You canna be expectin' money wi' the first. But we'll consuder, Colin. We'll paause and consuder."

Two days later the *Vital Spark* was going up to Inveraray for a cargo of timber, Para Handy steering, and singing softly to himself –

"As I gaed up yon Hieland hill,
 I met a bonny lassie;
She looked at me and I at her,
And oh, but she was saucy.
With my rolling eye,
Fal tee diddle dye,
Rolling eye dum derry,
With my rolling eye."

The Tar stood by him peeling potatoes, and the charming domestic sentiment of the song could not fail to suggest the subject of his recent thoughts. "Did you have time to consuder yon?" he asked the Captain, looking up at him with comical coyness.

"Am I no' consudering it as hard as I'm able?" said Para Handy. "Chust you swept aal them peelin's over the side and no' be spoiling the boat, my good laad."

"I wass mindin', mysel', of a femily of gyurls called Macphail up in Easdale, or maybe it wass Luing," said The Tar.

"Macphails!" cried Para Handy. "I never hear the name of Macphail but I need to scratch mysel'. I wouldna alloo any man on the *Fital Spark* to mairry a Macphail, even if she wass the Prunce of Wales. Look at that man of oors that caals himsel' an enchineer; he's a Macphail, that's the way he canna help it."

"Och, I wass chust in fun," The Tar hastened to say soothingly. "I don't think I would care for any of them Macphail gyurls whatever. Maybe you'll mind of something suitable before long."

Para Handy slapped himself on the knee. "My Chove!" said he, "I have the very article that would fit you."

"What's – what's her name?" asked The Tar alarmed at the way destiny seemed to be rushing him into matrimony.

"Man, I don't know," said the Captain, "but she's the laandry-maid up here in the Shurriff's – chust a regular beauty. I'll take you up and show her you to-morrow."

"Will we no' be awfu' busy to-morrow?" said The Tar hastily. "Maybe it would be better to wait till we come back again. There's no' an awfu' hurry."

"No hurry!" cried the Captain. "It's the poor heid for business you have, Colin; a gyurl the same as I'm thinkin' on for you will be snapped up whenever she gets her Mertinmas wages."

"I'm afraid she'll be too cluver for me, her being a laandry-maid," said The Tar. "They're aawfu' high-steppers, laandry-maids, and aawfu' stiff."

"That's wi' working among starch," explained Para Handy. "It'll aal come oot in the washin'. Not another word, Colin; leave it to me. And maybe Dougie, och ay, Dougie and me'll see you right."

So keenly did the Captain and Dougie enter into the matrimonial projects of The Tar that they did not even wait till the morrow, but set out to interview the young lady that evening. "I'll no' put on my pea-jecket or my watch-chain in case she might take a fancy to mysel'," the Captain said to his mate. "A man in a good poseetion like me canna be too caautious." The Tar, at the critical moment, showed the utmost reluctance to join the expedition. He hummed and hawed, protested he "didna like", and would prefer that they settled the business without him; but this was not according to Para Handy's ideas of business, and ultimately the three set out together with an arrangement that The Tar was to wait out in the Sheriff's garden while his ambassadors laid his suit in a preliminary form before a lady he had never set eyes on and who had never seen him.

There was a shower of rain, and the Captain and his mate had scarcely been ushered into the kitchen on a plea of "important business" by the Captain, than The Tar took shelter in a large wooden larder at the back of the house.

Para Handy and Dougie took a seat in the kitchen at the invitation of its single occupant, a stout cook with a humorous eye.

"It was the laandry-maid we were wantin' to see, mem," said the Captain, ducking his head forward several times and grinning widely to inspire confidence and create a genial atmosphere without any loss of time. "We were chust passing the door, and we thought we would give her a roar in the by-going."

"You mean Kate?" asked the cook.

"Ay! chust that, chust that – Kate," said the Captain, beaming warmly till his whiskers curled. "Hoo's the Shurriff keeping himsel'?" he added as an afterthought. "Iss he in good trum them days?" And he winked expansively at the cook.

" Kate's not in," said the domestic. "She'll be back in a while if you wait."

The Captain's face fell for a moment. "Och perhaps you'll do fine yoursel'," said he cordially, at last. "We have a fellow yonder on my boat that's come into some money, and what iss he determined on but to get mairried? He's aawfu' backward, for he never saw much Life except the Tarbert Fair, and he asked us to come up here and put in a word for him."

"Is that the way you do your courtin' on the coal-gabbarts?" said the cook, greatly amused.

"Coal-gaabert!" cried Para Handy, indignant. "There iss no coal-gaabert in the business; I am the Captain of the *Fital Spark*, the smertest steamboat in the coastin' tred –"

"And I'm no' slack mysel'; I'm the mate," said Dougie, wishing he had brought his trump.

"He must be a soft creature not to speak for himself," said the cook.

"Never mind that," said the Captain; "are you game to take him?"

The cook laughed. "What about yoursel'?" she asked chaffingly, and the Captain blenched.

"Me!" he cried. "I peety the wumman that would mairry me. If I wass not here, Dougie would tell you – would you no', Dougie? – I'm a fair duvvle for high jeenks. Forbye, I'm sometimes frightened for my health."

"And what is he like, this awfu' blate chap?" asked the cook.

"As smert a laad as ever stepped," protested Para Handy. "Us sailors iss sometimes pretty wild; it's wi' followin' the sea and fightin' hurricanes, here the day and away yesterday; but Colin iss ass dacent a laad ass ever came oot of Knapdale if he wass chust letting himself go. Dougie himsel' will tell you."

"There's nothing wrong wi' the fellow," said Dougie. "A fine riser in the mornin'."

"And for cookin', there's no' his equal," added the Captain.

"It seems to me it's my mistress you should have asked for," said the cook; "she's advertising for a scullery-maid." But this sarcasm passed over the heads of the eager ambassadors.

"Stop you!" said the Captain, "and I'll take him in himsel'; he's oot in the garden waiting on us." And he and the mate went outside.

"Colin!" cried Para Handy, "come away and be engaged, like a smert laad." But there was no answer, and it was after considerable searching they discovered the ardent suitor sound asleep in the larder.

"It's no' the laandry-maid; but it's a far bigger wan," explained the Captain. "She's chust sublime. Aal you have to do now is to come in and taalk nice to her."

The Tar protested he couldn't talk to her unless he had some conversation lozenges.

Besides, it was the laundry-maid he had arranged for, not the cook.

"She'll do fine for a start; a fine gyurl," the Captain assured him, and with some difficulty they induced The Tar to go with them to the back-door, only to find it emphatically shut in their faces.

"Let us paause and consuder, what day iss this?" asked the Captain, when the emphasis of the rebuff had got time to sink into his understanding.

"Friday," said Dougie.

"Tuts! wass I not sure of it? It's no' a lucky day for this kind of business. Never mind, Colin, we'll come to-morrow when the laandry-maid's in, and you'll bring a poke of conversation lozenges. You mustna be so stupid, man; you were awfu' tumid!"

"I wasna a bit tumid, but I wasna in trum," said The Tar, who was walking down to the quay with a curious and unusual straddle.

"And what for would you not come at wance when I cried you in?" asked the Captain.

"Because," said The Tar pathetically, "I had a kind of an accident yonder in the larder: I sat doon on a basket of country eggs."

14

PARA HANDY'S PIPER

IF you haven't been at your favourite coast resort except at the time of summer holidays, you don't know much about it. At other seasons of the year it looks different, smells different, and sounds different – that is, when there's any sound at all in it. In those dozing, dreamy days before you come down with your yellow tin trunk or your kit-bag, there's only one sound in the morning in the coast resort – the sizzling of frying herring. If it is an extra lively day, you may also hear the baker's van-driver telling a dead secret to the deaf bellman at the other end of the village, and the cry of sea-gulls. Peace broods on that place then like a benediction, and (by the odour) some one is having a sheep's head singed at the smithy.

I was standing one day on Brodick quay with Para Handy when the place looked so vacant, and was so quiet we unconsciously talked in whispers for fear of wakening somebody. The *Vital Spark* shared the peace of that benign hour: she nodded idly at the quay, her engineer half asleep with a penny novelette in his hands; The Tar, sound asleep and snoring, unashamed, with his back against the winch; Dougie, the mate, smoking in silent solemnity, and occasionally scratching his nose, otherwise you would bave taken him for an ingenious automatic smoking-machine, set agoing by putting a penny in the slot. If anybody had dropped a postage-stamp in Brodick that day, it would have sounded like a dynamite explosion. It was the breakfast hour.

Suddenly a thing happened that seemed to rend the very heavens: it was the unexpected outburst of a tinker piper, who came into sight round the corner of a house, with his instrument in the preliminary stages of the attack.

"My Chove!" said Para Handy, "isn't that fine? Splendid aalthegither!"

"What's your favourite instrument?" I asked.

"When Dougie's in trum it's the trump," said he in a low voice, lest the mate (who was certainly very vain of his skill on the trump – that is to say, the Jew's harp) should hear him; "but, man! for gaiety, the pipes. They're truly sublime! A trump's fine for small occasions, but for style you need the pipes. And good pipers iss difficult nooadays to get; there's not many in it. You'll maybe can get a kind of a plain piper going aboot the streets of Gleska noo and then, but they're like the herrin', and the turnips, and rhubarb, and things like that – you don't get them fresh in Gleska; if you want them at their best, you have to go up to the right Hielands and pull them off the tree. You ken what I mean yoursel'."

And the Captain of the *Vital Spark* widely opened his mouth and inhaled the sound of the bagpipe with an air of great refreshment.

"That's 'The Barren Rocks of Aden' he iss on now," he informed me by and by. "I can tell by the sound of it. Oh, music! music! it's me that's fond of it. It makes me feel that droll I could bound over the mountains, if you understand. Do you know that I wance had a piper of my own?"

"A piper of your own!"

"Ay, chust that, a piper of my own, the same ass if I wass the Marquis of Bute. You'll be thinkin' I couldna afford it," Para Handy went on, smiling slyly, "but a Macfarlane never wass bate. Aal the fine gentry hass their piper that plays to them in the mornin' to put them up, and goes playin' roond the table at dinner-time when there's any English vusitors there, and let them chust take it! It serves them right; they should stay in their own country. My piper wass a Macdonald."

"You mean one of the tinker pipers?" I said mischievously, for I knew a tribe of tinker pipers of that name.

Para Handy was a little annoyed. "Well," he said, "I wouldna deny but he wass a kind of a tinker, but he wass in the Militia when he wass workin', and looked quite smert when he wass sober."

"How long did you keep the piper?" I asked, really curious about this unexpected incident in the Captain's career.

"Nearly a whole day," he answered. "Whiles I kept him and whiles he wass going ashore for a dram.

"To let you understand, it wass the time of the fine fushin's in Loch Fyne, and I had a cousin yonder that wass gettin' mairried at Kilfinan. The weddin' wass to be on a Friday, and I wass passin' up the loch with a cargo of salt, when my cousin hailed me from the shore, and came oot in a small boat to speak to me.

" 'Peter,' he said to me, quite bashful, 'they're sayin' I'm goin' to get mairried on Friday, and I'm lookin' for you to be at the thing.'

" 'You can depend on me bein' there, Dougald,' I assured him. 'It would be a poor thing if the Macfarlanes would not stick by wan another at a time of trial.'

" 'Chust that!' said my cousin; 'there's to be sixteen hens on the table and plenty of refreshment. What's botherin' me iss that there's not a piper in Kilfinan. I wass thinkin' that maybe between this and Friday you would meet wan on your trevels, and take him back with you on your shup.'

" 'Mercy on us! You would think it wass a parrot from foreign perts I wass to get for you,' I said. 'But I'll do my best,' and off we went. I watched the hillsides aal the way up the loch to see if I could see a piper; but it wass the time of the year when there's lots of work at the hay, and the pipers wass keepin' oot of sight, till I came to Cairndow. Dougie and me wass ashore at Cairndow in the mornin', when we saw this Macdonald I'm telling you aboot standin' in front of the Inns with pipes under his oxter. He wass not playin' them at the time. I said to him, 'There's a weddin' yonder at Kilfinan to-morrow, that they're wantin' a piper for. What would you take to come away doon on my vessel and play for them?'

" 'Ten shillin's and my drink,' he said, as quick as anything.

" 'Say five and it's a bargain,' I said; and he engaged himself on the spot. He wass a great big fellow with a tartan trooser and a cocketty bonnet, and oh, my goodness! but his hair wass rud! I couldna but offer him a dram before we left Cairndow, for we were startin' there and then, but he wouldna set foot in the Inns, and we went on board the *Fital Spark* withoot anything at all, and started doon the loch. I thought it wass a droll kind of a piper I had that would lose a chance.

"When we would be a mile or two on the passage, I said to him, 'Macdonald, tune up your pipes and give us the Macfarlanes' Merch.'

"He said he didna know the Macfarlanes had a Merch, but would do the best he could by the ear, and hc began to screw the bits of his pipes together. It took him aboot an hour, and by that time we were off Strachur.

" 'Stop you the boat,' he said, 'I'll need to get ashore a meenute to get something to soften the bag of this pipes; it's ass hard ass a bit of stick.'

" 'You can get oil from the enchineer,' I said to him.

" 'Oil!' said he; 'do you think it's a clock I'm mendin'? No,

no; there's nothing will put a pipe bag in trum but some treacle poured in by the stock.'

"Well, we went ashore and up to the Inns, and he asked if they could give him treacle for his bagpipes. They said they had none. 'Weel,' said he, 'next to that the best thing for it iss whusky – give me a gill of the best, and the Captain here will pay for it; I'm his piper.' He got the gill, and what did he do but pour a small sensation of it into the inside of his pipes and drink the rest? 'It comes to the same thing in the long-run,' said he, and we got aboard again, and away we started.

" 'There's another tune I am very fond of,' I said to him, watchin' him workin' away puttin' his drones in order. 'It's "The 93rd's Farewell to Gibraltar".'

" 'I ken it fine,' he said, 'but I don't ken the tune. Stop you, and I'll give you a trate if I could get this cursed pipe in order. What aboot the dinner?'

"The dinner wass nearly ready, so he put the pipes past till he wass done eatin', and then he had a smoke, and by the time that wass done we were off Lochgair. 'That puts me in mind,' said he; 'I wonder if I could get a chanter reed from Maclaclan the innkeeper? He plays the pipes himself. The chanter reed I have iss bad, and I would like to do the best I could at your cousin's weddin'.'

"We stopped, and Dougie went ashore in the smaal boat with him, and when they came back in half-an-hour the piper said it wass a peety, but the innkeeper wasna a piper efter aal, and didna have a reed, but maybe we would get wan in Ardrishaig.

" 'We're no' goin' to Ardrishaig, we're goin' to Kilfinan,' I told him, and he said he couldna help it, but we must make for Ardrishaig, right or wrong, for he couldna play the pipes right withoot a new reed. 'When you hear me playing,' he said, 'you will be glad you took the trouble. There iss not my equal in the three parishes,' and, man, but his hair wass rud, rud!

"We wouldna be half-an-oor oot from Lochgair when he asked if the tea would soon be ready. He wass that busy puttin' his pipes in order, he said, he was quite fatigued. Pipers iss like canaries, you have to keep them going weel with meat and drink if you want music from them. We gave him his tea, and by the time it wass finished we were off Ardrishaig, and he made me put her in there to see if he could get a reed for his chanter. Him and Dougie went ashore in the smaal boat. Dougie came back in an 'oor wi' his hair awfu' tousy and nobody wi' him.

" 'Where's my piper?' I said to him.

" 'Man, it's terrible!' said Dougie; 'the man's no a piper at aal, and he's away on the road to Kilmertin. When he wass standin' at Cairndow Inns yonder, he was chust holdin' the pipes for a man that wass inside for his mornin', and you and me'll maybe get into trouble for helpin' him to steal a pair o' pipes.'

"That wass the time I kept a piper of my own," said Para Handy, in conclusion. "And Dougie had to play the trump to the dancin' at my cousin's weddin'."

15

THE SAILORS AND THE SALE

PARA HANDY'S great delight was to attend farm sales. "A sale's a sublime thing," he said, "for if you don't like a thing you don't need to buy it. It's at the sales a good many of the other vessels in the tred get their sailors." This passion for sales was so strong in him that if there was one anywhere within twelve miles of any port the *Vital Spark* was lying at, he would lose a tide or risk demurrage rather than miss it. By working most part of a night he got a cargo of coals discharged at Lochgoilhead one day in time to permit of his attending a displenishing sale ten miles away. He and the mate, Dougie, started in a brake that was conveying people to the sale; they were scarcely half-way there when the Captain sniffed.

"Hold on a meenute and listen, Dougie," said he. "Do you no' smell anything?"

Dougie sniffed too, and his face was lit up by a beautiful smile as of one who recognises a friend. "It's not lemon kali at any rate," he said knowingly, and chuckled in his beard.

"Boys!" said the Captain, turning round to address the other passengers in the brake, who were mainly cattle dealers and farmers – "Boys! this iss going to be a majestic sale; we're five miles from the place and I can smell the whisky already."

At that moment the driver of the brake bent to look under his seat, and looked up again with great vexation written on his countenance. "Isn't it not chust duvvelish?" he said. "Have I not gone away and put my left foot through a bottle of good spurits I wass bringing up wi' me in case anybody would take ill through the night."

"Through the night! " exclaimed one of the farmers, who was plainly not long at the business. "What night are you taalking aboot?"

"This night," replied the driver promptly.

"But surely we'll be back at Lochgoilhead before night?" said the farmer, and all the others in the coach looked at him with mingled pity and surprise.

"It's a ferm sale we're going to, and not a rent collection," said the driver. "And there's thirty-six gallons of ale ordered for it, no' to speak of refreshments. If we're home in time for breakfast from this sale it's me that'll be the bonny surprised man, I'm telling you."

At these farm sales old custom demands that food and drink should be supplied "ad lib." by the outgoing tenant. It costs money, but it is a courtesy that pays in the long-run, for if the bidding hangs fire a brisk circulation of the refreshments stimulates competition among the buyers, and

adds twenty per cent to the price of stots. It would be an injustice to Para Handy and Dougie to say they attended sales from any consideration of this sort; they went because of the high jeenks. At the close of the day sometimes they found that they had purchased a variety of things not likely to be of much use on board a steam-lighter, as on the occasion when Dougie bought the rotary churn.

"Keep away from the hoosehold furniture aalthegither!" said the Captain, this day. "We have too mich money in oor pockets between us, and it'll be safer no' to be in sight of the unctioneer till the beasts iss on, for we'll no' be tempted to buy beasts."

"I would buy an elephant for the fun of the thing, let alone a coo or two," said Dougie.

"That's put me in mind," said the Captain, "there's a cousin of my own yonder in Kilfinan wantin' a milk coo for the last twelvemonth; if I saw a bargain maybe I would take it. But we'll do nothing rash, Dougie, nothing rash; maybe we're chust sailors, but we're no' daft aalthegither."

By this time they were standing on the outside of a crowd of prospective purchasers interested

in a collection of farm utensils and household sundries, the disposal of which preceded the rouping of the beasts. The forenoon was chilly; the chill appeared to affect the mood of the crowd, who looked coldly on the chain harrows, turnip-cutters, and other articles offered to them at prices which the auctioneer said it broke his heart to mention, and it was to instil a little warmth into the proceedings that a handy man with red whiskers went round with refreshments on a tray.

"Streetch your hand and take a gless," he said to the Captain. "It'll do you no herm."

"Man, I'm not mich caring for it," drawled the Captain. "I had wan yesterday. What do you think, Dougie? Would it do any herm chust to take wan gless to show we're freendly to the sale of impliments and things?"

"Whatever you say yoursel'," replied Dougie diffidently, but at the same time grasping the glass nearest him with no uncertain hand.

"Weel, here's good prices!" said the Captain, fixing to another glass, and after that the sun seemed to come out with a genial glow.

The lamentable fact must be recorded that before the beasts came up to the hammer the mate of the *Vital Spark* had become possessor of a pair of curling-stones – one of them badly chipped – a Dutch hoe, and a baking-board.

"What in the world are you going to do with that trash?" asked the Captain, returning from a visit to the outhouse where the ale was, to find his mate with the purchases at his feet.

"Och! it's aal right," said Dougie, cocking his eye at him. "I wassna giving a docken for the things mysel', but I saw the unctioneer aye look-looking at me, and I didna like no' to take nothing. It's chust, as you might say, for the good of the hoose. Stop you and you'll see some fun."

"But it's a rideeculous thing buying curling-stones at this time of the year, and you no' a curler. What?"

Dougie scratched his neck and looked at his purchases. "They didn't cost mich," he said; "and they're aye handy to have aboot you."

When the cattle came under the hammer it was discovered that prices were going to be very low. All the likely buyers seemed to be concentrated round the beer-barrel in the barn, with the result that stots, queys, cows, and calves were going at prices that brought the tears to the auction-eer's eyes. He hung so long on the sale of one particular cow for which he could only squeeze out offers up to five pounds that Para Handy took pity on him, and could not resist giving a nod that put ten shillings on to its price and secured the animal.

"Name, please?" said the auctioneer, cheering up wonderfully.

"Captain Macfarlane," said Para Handy, and, very much distressed at his own impetuosity, took his mate aside. "There you are, I bought your coo for you," he said to Dougie.

"For me!" exclaimed his mate. "What in the world would I be doing with a coo?"

"You said yoursel' you would take a coo or two for the fun o' the thing," said Para Handy.

"When I'm buying coos I'm buying them by my own word o' mooth; you can chust keep it for

your cousin in Kilfinan. If I wass buyin' a coo it wouldna be wan you could hang your hat on in fifty places. No, no, Peter, I'm Hielan', but I'm no' so Hielan' ass aal that."

"My goodness!" said Para Handy, "this iss the scrape! I will have to be taking her to Lochgoilhead, and hoisting her on the vessel, and milking her, and keeping her goodness knows what time till I'll have a cargo the length of Kilfinan. Forbye, my cousin and me's no' speakin' since Whitsunday last."

"Go up to the unctioneer and tell him you didna buy it at aal, that you were only noddin' because you had a tight collar," suggested the mate, and the Captain acted on the suggestion; but the auctioneer was not to be taken in by any such story, and Para Handy and his mate were accordingly seen on the road to Lochgoil late that night with a cow, the possession of which took all the pleasure out of their day's outing. Dougie's curling-stones, hoe, and baking-board were to follow in a cart.

It was a long time after this before the *Vital Spark* had any occasion to go to Lochgoilhead. Macphail the engineer had only to mention the name of the place and allude casually to the price of beef or winter feeding, and the Captain would show the most extraordinary ill-temper. The fact was he had left his purchase at a farmer's at Lochgoil to keep for him till called for, and he never liked to think upon the day of reckoning. But the *Vital Spark* had to go to Lochgoilhead sooner or later, and the first time she did so the Captain went somewhat mournfully up to the farm where his cow was being kept for him.

"It's a fine day; hoo's the mustress?" he said to the farmer, who showed some irritation at never having heard from the owner of the cow for months.

"Fine, but what aboot your coo, Peter?"

"My Chove! iss she living yet?" said the Captain. "I'll be due you a penny or two."

"Five pounds, to be exact; and it'll be five pounds ten at the end of next month."

"Chust the money I paid for her," said Para Handy. "Chust you keep her for me till the end of next month, and then pay yoursel' with her when my account iss up to the five pound ten," a bargain which was agreed on; and so ended Para Handy's most expensive high jeenk.

16

A NIGHT ALARM

THE wheel of the *Vital Spark* was so close to the engines that the Captain could have given his orders in a whisper, but he was so proud of the boat that he liked to sail her with all the honours, so he always used the knocker. He would catch the brass knob and give one, two, or three knocks as the circumstances demanded, and then put his mouth to the speaking-tube and cry coaxingly down to the engineer, "Stop her, Dan, when you're ready." That would be when she was a few lengths off the quay. Dan, the engineer, never let on he heard the bell; he was very fond of reading penny novelettes, and it was only when he was spoken to soothingly down the tube that he would put aside "Lady Winifred's Legacy", give a sigh, and stop his engine. Then he would stand upright – which brought his head over the level of the deck, and beside the Captain's top-boots – wiping his brow with a piece of waste the way real engineers do on the steamers that go to America. His great aim in taking a quay was to suggest to anybody hanging about it that it was frightfully hot in the engine-room – just like the Red Sea – while the fact was that most of the time there was a draught in the engine-room of the *Vital Spark* that would keep a cold store going without ice.

When he stuck up his head he always said to the Captain, "You're aye wantin' something or other; fancy goin' awa' and spoilin' me in the middle o' a fine baur."

"I'm sorry, Dan," Para Handy would say to him in an agony of remorse, for he was afraid of

the engineer because that functionary had once been on a ship that made a voyage to Australia, and used to say he had killed a man in the Bush. When he was not sober it was two men, and he would weep. "I'm sorry, Dan, but I did not know you would be busy." Then he would knock formally to reverse the engine, and cry down the tube, "Back her, Dan, when you're ready; there's no hurry," though the engineer was, as I have said, so close that he could have put his hand on his head.

Dan drew in his head, did a bit of juggling with the machinery, and resumed his novelette at the place where Lady Winifred lost her jewels at the ball. There was something breezy in the way he pulled in his head and moved in the engine-room that disturbed the Captain. "Dan's no' in good trum the day," he would say, in a hoarse whisper to the mate Dougie under these circumstances. "You daurna say wan word to him but he flies in a tiravee."

"It's them cursed novelles," was always Dougie's explanation; "they would put any man wrong in the heid, let alone an enchineer. If it wass me wass skipper of this boat, I wadna be so soft with him, I'll assure you."

"Ach, you couldna be hard on the chap and him a Macphail," said the Captain. "There wass never any holdin' o' them in. He's an aawful fellow for high jeenks; he killed a man in the Bush."

One afternoon the *Vital Spark* came into Tarbert with a cargo of coals that could not be discharged till the morning, for Sandy Sinclair's horse and cart were engaged at a country funeral. The Captain hinted at repainting a strake or two of the vessel, but his crew said they couldn't be bothered, forbye Dougie had three shillings; so they washed their faces after tea and went up the town. Peace brooded on the *Vital Spark*, though by some overlook Macphail had left her with almost a full head of steam. Sergeant Macleod, of the constabulary, came down when she lay deserted. "By Cheorge!" said he to himself, "them fellows iss coing to get into trouble this night, I'm tellin' you," for he knew the *Vital Spark* of old. He drew his tippit more firmly about him, breathed hard, and went up the town to survey the front of all the public-houses. Peace brooded on the *Vital Spark* – a benign and beautiful calm.

It was ten o'clock at night when her crew returned. They came down the quay in a condition which the most rigid moralist could only have described as jovial, and went to their bunks in the fo'c'sle. A drizzling rain was falling. That day the Captain had mounted a new cord on the steam whistle, so that he could blow it by a jerk from his position at the wheel. It was drawn back taut, and the free end of it was fastened to a stanchion. As the night passed and the rain continued falling, the cord contracted till at last it acted on the whistle, which opened with a loud and croupy hoot that rang through the harbour and over the town. Otherwise peace still brooded on the *Vital Spark*. It took fifteen minutes to waken the Captain, and he started up in wild alarm. His crew were snoring in the light of a small globe lamp, and the engineer had a "Family Herald Supplement" on his chest.

"That's either some duvvlement of somebody's or a warnin'," said Para Handy, half irritated, half in superstitious alarm. "Dougie, are you sleepin'?"

"What would I be here for if I wass not sleepin'?" said Dougie.

"Go up like a smert laad and see who's meddlin' my whustle."

"I canna," said Dougie; "I havena but the wan o' my boots on. Send up The Tar." The Tar was so plainly asleep from his snoring that it seemed no use to tackle him. The Captain looked at him. "Man!" he said, "he hass a nose that minds me o' a winter day, it's so short and dirty. He would be no use any way. It's the enchineer's chob, but I daurna waken him, he's such a man for high jeenks." And still the whistle waked the echoes of Tarbert.

"If I wass skipper of this boat I would show him," said Dougie, turning in his bunk, but showing no sign of any willingness to turn out. "Give him a roar, Peter, or throw the heel of yon pan loaf at him."

"I would do it in a meenute if he wasna a Macphail," said the Captain, distracted. "He wance killed a man in the Bush. But he's the enchineer; the whustle's in his depairtment. Maybe if I spoke nice to him he would see aboot it. Dan!" he cried softly across the fo'c'sle to the man with the "Family Herald Supplement" on his chest – "Dan, show a leg, like a good laad, and go up and stop that cursed whustle."

"Are you speakin' to me?" said the engineer, who was awake all the time.

"I was chust makin' a remark," explained the Captain hurriedly. "It's not of any great import-ance, but there's a whustle there, and it's wakin' the whole toon of Tarbert. If you werena awfu' throng sleepin', you might take a bit turn on dake and see what is't. Chust when you're ready, Dan, chust when you're ready."

Dan ostentatiously turned on his side and loudly went to sleep again. And the whistle roared louder than ever.

The Captain began to lose his temper. "Stop you till I get back to Bowling," he said, "and I'll give every man of you the whole jeeng-bang, and get rale men for the *Fital Spark*. Not a wan of you iss worth a spittle in the hour of dancher and trial. Look at Macphail there tryin' to snore like an enchineer with a certeeficate, and him only a fireman! I am not a bit frightened for him; I do not believe he ever killed a man in the Bush at aal – he hass not the game for it; I'll bate you he never wass near Australia – and what wass his mother but wan of the Macleans of Kenmore? Chust that; wan of the Macleans of Kenmore! Him and his pride! If I had my Sunday clothes on I would give him my opeenion. And there you are, Dougie! I thocht you were a man and not a mice. You are lying there in your ignorance, and never wass the length of Ullapool. Look at me – on the vessels three over twenty years, and twice wrecked in the North at places that's not on the maps."

The two worthies thus addressed paid no attention and snored with suspicious steadiness, and the Captain turned his attention to The Tar.

"Colin!" he said more quietly, "show a leg, like a cluvver fellow, and go up and put on the fire for the breakfast." But The Tar made no response, and in the depth of the fo'c'sle Para Handy's angry voice rose up again, as he got out of his bunk and prepared to pull on some clothes and go up on deck himself.

"Tar by by-name and Tar by nature!" said he. "You will stick to your bed that hard they could not take you off without half-a-pound of saalt butter. My goodness! have I not a bonny crew? You are chust a wheen of crofters. When the owners of vessels wass wantin' men like you, they go to the Kilmichael cattle-market and drag you down with a rope to the seaside. You will not do the wan word I tell you. I'll wudger I'll not hammer down to you again, Dan, or use the speakin'-tube, the same ass if you were a rale enchineer – I'll chust touch you with the toe of my boot when I want you to back her, mind that! There iss not a finer nor a faster vessel than the *Fital Spark* in the tred; she iss chust sublime, and you go and make a fool of her with your drinking and your laziness and your ignorance."

He got up on deck in a passion, to find a great many Tarbert people running down the quay to see what was wrong, and Sergeant Macleod at the head of them.

"Come! come! Peter, what iss this whustlin' for on a wet night like this at two o'clock in the mornin'?" asked the sergeant, with a foot on the bulwark. "What are you blow-blow-blowin' at your whustle like that for?"

"Chust for fun," said the Captain. "I'm a terrible fellow for high jeenks. I have three fine stots from the Kilmichael market down below here, and they canna sleep unless they hear a whustle."

"The man's in the horrors!" said the sergeant in a whisper to some townsmen beside him on the quay. "I must take him to the lock-up and make a case of him, and it's no' a very nice chob, for he's ass strong ass a horse. Wass I not sure there would be trouble when I saw the *Fital Spark* the day? It must be the lock-up for him, and maybe Lochgilphead, but it iss a case for deleeber-ation and caaution – great caaution."

"Captain Macfarlane," he said in a bland voice to the Captain, who stood defiant on the deck, making no attempt to stop the whistling. "Mr Campbell the banker wass wantin' to see you for a meenute up the toon. Chust a meenute! He asked me to come doon and tell you."

"What will the banker be wantin' wi' me?" said the Captain, cooling down and suspecting nothing. "It's a droll time o' night to be sendin' for onybody."

"So it is, Captain Macfarlane," admitted the constable mildly. "I do not know exactly what he wants, but it iss in a great hurry. He said he would not keep you wan meenute. I think it will be to taalk about your cousin Cherlie's money."

"I'll go wi' you whenever I get on my bonnet," said the Captain, preparing to go below.

"Never mind your bonnet; it iss chust a step or two, and you'll be back in five meenutes," said the sergeant; and, thus cajoled, the Captain of the *Vital Spark*, having cut the cord and stopped the whistle, went lamb-like to the police office.

Peace fell again upon the *Vital Spark*.

17

A DESPERATE CHARACTER

THOUGH Para Handy went, like a lamb, with Sergeant Macleod, he had not to suffer the ignominy of the police office, for the sergeant found out on the way that the Captain belonged to the Wee Free, and that made a great deal of difference. Instead of putting the mariner into a cell, he took him into his own house, made a summary investigation into the cause of the whistling of the *Vital Spark*, found the whole thing was an accident, dismissed the accused without a stain on his character, gave him a dram, and promised to take him down a pair of white hares for a present before the vessel left Tarbert.

"I am glad to see you belong to the right Church, Peter," he said. "Did I not think you were chust wan of them unfuduls that carries the rud-edged hime-books and sits at the prayer, and here you are chust a dacent Christian like mysel'. My goodness! It shows you a man cannot be too caautious. Last year there wass but a small remnant of us Christians to the fore here – myself and Macdougall the merchant, and myself and the Campbells up in Clonary Farm, and myself and the steamboat aagent, and myself and my cousins at Dunmore; but it'll be changed days when we get a ha'ad o' the church. They'll be sayin' there's no hell; we'll show them, I'll assure you! We are few, but firm – firm; there's no bowin' of the knee with us, and many a pair of white hares I'll be gettin' from the Campbells up in Clonary. I have chust got to say the word that wan of the rale old Frees iss in a vessel at the quay, and there will be a pair of white hares doon for you to-morrow."

"I'm a staunch Free," said Para Handy, upsetting his glass, which by this time had hardly a drop left in it. "Tut! tut!" he exclaimed apologetically, "it's a good thing I never broke the gless. Stop! stop! stop in a meenute; I'm sure I'm no needin' any more. But it's a cold wet nicht, whatever. I'm a staunch Free. I never had a hime-book on board my boat; if Dougie wass here he would tell you."

"You'll no' get very often to the church, wi' you goin' about from place to place followin' the sea?" said the sergeant.

"That's the worst of it," said Para Handy, heaving a tremendous sigh. "There's no mich fun on a coal vessel; if it wasna the *Fital Spark* wass the smertest in the tred, and me the skipper of her, I would mairry a fine strong wife and start a business. There wass wan time yonder, when I wass younger, I wass very keen to be a polisman."

"The last chob!" cried the sergeant. "The very last chob on earth! You would be better to be trapping rabbits. It iss not an occupation for any man that has a kind he'rt, and I have a he'rt mysel' that's no slack in that direction, I'm tellin' you. Many a time I'll have to take a poor laad in and cherge him, and he'll be fined, and it's mysel' that's the first to get the money for his fine."

"Do you tell me you pay the fine oot of your own pocket?" asked Para Handy, astonished.

"Not a bit of it; I have aal my faculties about me. I go roond and raise a subscruption," explained the sergeant. "I chust go roond and say the poor laad didna mean any herm, and his mother wass a weedow, and it iss aal right, och aye! it iss aal right at wance wi' the folk in Tarbert. Kind, kind he'rts in Tarbert – if there's any fushing. But the polis iss no chob for a man like me. Still and on it's a good pay, and the uniform, and a fine pair of boots, and an honour, so I'm no' complaining. Not a bit!"

Para Handy put up his hand with his customary gesture to scratch his ear, but as usual thought better of it, and sheered off. "Do you ken oor Dougie?" he asked.

"Iss it your mate?" replied the constable. "They're telling me aboot him, but I never had him in my hands."

"It's easy seen you're no' long in Tarbert," said the Captain. "He wass wan time namely here

for makin' trouble; but that wass before he wass a kind of a Rechabite. Did you hear aboot him up in Castlebay in Barra?"

"No," said the sergeant.

"Dougie will be aye bouncin' he wass wan time on the yats, and wearing a red night-kep aal the time, and whitening on his boots, the same ass if he wass a doorstep, but, man! he's tumid, tumid! If there's a touch of a gale he starts at his prayers, and says he'll throw his trump over the side. He can play the trump sublime – reels and things you never heard the like of; and if he wass here, and him in trum, it's himself would show you. But when the weather's scoury, and the *Fital Spark* not at the quay, he'll make up his mind to live a better life, and the first thing that he's going to stop's the trump. 'Hold you on, Dougie,' I'll be sayin' to him; 'don't do anything desperate till we see if the weather'll no lift on the other side of Minard.' It's a long way from Oban out to Barra; many a man that hass gold braid on his kep in the Clyde never went so far, but it's nothing at aal to the *Fital Spark*. But Dougie does not like that trup at aal, at aal. Give him Bowling to Blairmore in the month of Aagust, and there's no' a finer sailor ever put on oilskins."

"Och, the poor fellow!" said the sergeant, with true sympathy.

"Stop you!" proceeded Para Handy. "When we would be crossing the Munch, Dougie would be going to sacrifice his trump, and start releegion every noo and then; but when we had the vessel tied to the quay at Castlebay, the merchants had to shut their shops and make a holiday."

"My Chove! do you tell me?" cried the sergeant.

"If Dougie was here himsel' he would tell you," said the Captain. "It needed but the wan or two drams, and Dougie would start walkin' on his heels to put an end to Castlebay. There iss not many shops in the place aalthegither, and the shopkeepers are aal MacNeils, and cousins to wan another; so when Dougie was waalkin' on his heels and in trum for high jeenks, they had a taalk together, and agreed it would be better chust to put on the shutters."

"Isn't he the desperate character!" said the constable. "Could they no' have got the polis?"

"There's no a polisman in the island of Barra," said Para Handy. "If there wass any need for polismen they would have to send to Lochmaddy, and it would be two or three days before they could put Dougie on his trial. Forbye, they kent Dougie fine; they hadna any ill-wull to the laad, and maybe it wass a time there wasna very mich business doin' anyway. When Dougie would find the shops shut he would be as vexed as anything, and make for the school. He would go into the school and give the children a lecture on music and the curse of drink, with illustrations on the trump. At last they used to shut the school, too, and give the weans a holiday, whenever the *Fital Spark* was seen off Castle Kismul. He wass awfu' popular, Dougie, wi' the weans in Castlebay."

"A man like that should not be at lerge," said the constable emphatically.

"Och! he wass only in fun; there wass no more herm in Dougie than a fly. Chust fond of high jeenks and recreation; many a place in the Highlands would be gled to get the lend of him to keep them cheery in the winter-time. There's no herm in Dougie, not at aal, chust a love of sport and recreation. If he wass here himsel' he would tell you."

"It iss a good thing for him he does not come to Tarbert for his recreation," said the constable sternly; "we're no' so Hielan' in Tarbert ass to shut the shops when a man iss makin' himsel' a nuisance. By Cheorge! if he starts any of his high jeenks in Tarbert he'll suffer the Laaw."

"There iss no fear of Tarbert nowadays," said the Captain, "for Dougie iss a changed man. He mairried a kind of a wife yonder at Greenock, and she made him a Good Templar, or a Rechabite, or something of the sort where you get ten shillin's a week if your leg's broken fallin' doon the stair, and nobody saw you. Dougie's noo a staunch teetotaller except aboot the time of the old New Year, or when he'll maybe be takin' a dram for medicine. It iss a good thing for his wife, but it leaves an awfu' want in Barra and them other places where they kent him in his best trum."

18

THE TAR'S WEDDING

IT was months after The Tar's consultation with Para Handy about a wife: The Tar seemed to have given up the idea of indulgence in any such extravagance, and Para Handy had ceased to recommend various "smert, muddle-aged ones wi' a puckle money" to the consideration of the young man, when the latter one day sheepishly approached him, spat awkwardly through the clefts of his teeth at a patch in the funnel of the *Vital Spark*, and remarked, "I wass thinkin' to mysel' yonder, Captain, that if there wass nothing parteecular doing next Setturday, I would maybe get mairried."

"Holy smoke!" said the Captain; "you canna expect me to get a wife suitable for you in that time. It's no reasonable. Man, you're gettin' droll – chust droll!"

"Och, I needn't be puttin' you to any trouble," said The Tar, rubbing the back of his neck with a hand as rough as a rasp. "I wass lookin' aboot mysel', and there's wan yonder in Campbeltown'll have me. In fact, it's settled. I thocht that when we were in Campbeltown next Setturday, we could do the chob and be dune wi't. We were roared last Sunday –"

"Roared!" said the Captain. "Iss it cried, you mean?"

"Yes, chust cried," said The Tar, "but the gyurl's kind of dull in the hearing, and it would likely need to be a roar. You'll maybe ken her – she's wan of the MacCallums."

"A fine gyurl," said the Captain, who had not the faintest idea of her identity, and had never set eyes on her, but could always be depended on for politeness. "A fine gyurl! Truly sublime! I'm not askin' if there's any money; eh? – not a word! It's none of my business, but, tuts! what's the money anyway, when there's love?"

"Shut up aboot that!" said the scandalised Tar, getting very red. "If you're goin' to speak aboot love, be dacent and speak aboot it in the Gaalic. But we're no' taalkin' aboot love; we're taalkin' aboot my merrage. Is it aal right for Setturday?"

"You're a cunning man to keep it dark till this," said the Captain, "but I'll put nothing in the way, seein' it's your first caper of the kind. We'll have high jeenks at Campbeltown."

The marriage took place in the bride's mother's house, up a stair that was greatly impeded by festoons of fishing-nets, old oars, and net-bows on the walls, and the presence of six stalwart Tarbert trawlers, cousins of The Tar's, who were asked to the wedding, but were so large and had so many guernseys on, they would of themselves have filled the room in which the ceremony took place; so they had agreed, while the minister was there at all events, to take turn about of going in to countenance the proceedings. What space there was within was monopolised by the relatives of the bride, by Para Handy and Dougie, The Tar in a new slop-shop serge suit, apparently cut out by means of a hatchet, the bride – a good deal prettier than a Goth like The Tar deserved – and the minister. The wedding-supper was laid out in a neighbour's house on the same stair-landing.

A solemn hush marked the early part of the proceedings, marred only by the sound of something frying in the other house and the shouts of children crying for bowl-money in the street. The minister was a teetotaller, an unfortunate circumstance which the Captain had discovered very early, and he was very pleased with the decorum of the company. The MacCallums were not church-goers in any satisfactory sense, but they and their company seemed to understand what was duc to a Saturday night marriage and the presence of "the cloth". The clergyman had hardly finished the ceremony when the Captain began manoevring for his removal. He had possessed himself of a bottle of ginger cordial and a plate of cake.

"You must drink the young couple's health, Mr Grant," he said. "We ken it's you that's the busy man on the Setturday night, and indeed it's a night for the whole of us goin' home early. I have a ship yonder, the *Fital Spark*, that I left in cherge of an enchineer by the name of Macphail, no' to be trusted with such a responsibulity."

The minister drank the cheerful potion, nibbled the corner of a piece of cake, and squeezed his way downstairs between the Tarbert trawlers.

"We're chust goin' away oorsel's in ten meenutes," said the Captain after him.

"Noo that's aal right," said Para Handy, who in virtue of his office had constituted himself master of ceremonies. "He's a nice man, Mr Grant, but he's not strong, and it would be a peety to be keeping him late out of his bed on a Setturday night. I like, mysel', yon old-fashioned munisters that had nothing wrong wi' them, and took a Christian dram. Pass oot that bottle of chinger cordial to the laads from Tarbert and you'll see fine fun."

He was the life and soul of the evening after that. It was he who pulled the corks, who cut the cold ham, who kissed the bride first, who sang the first song, and danced with the new mother-in-law. "You're an aawful man, Captain Macfarlane," she said in fits of laughter at his fun.

"Not me!" said he, lumberingly dragging her round in a polka to the strains of Dougie's trump. "I'm a quate fellow, but when I'm in trum I like a high jeenk noo and then. Excuse my feet. It's no' every day we're merryin' The Tar. A fine, smert, handy fellow, Mrs MacCallum; you didn't make a bad bargain of it with your son-in-law. Excuse my feet. A sailor every inch of him, once you get him wakened. A pound a-week of wages an' no incumbrance. My feet again, excuse them!"

"It's little enough for two," said Mrs MacCallum; "but a man's aye a man," and she looked the Captain in the eye with disconcerting admiration.

"My Chove! she's a weedow wuman," thought the Captain; "I'll have to ca' canny, or I'll be in for an engagement."

"I aye liked sailors," said Mrs MacCallum; "John – that's the depairted, I'm his relic – was wan."

"A poor life, though," said the Captain, "especially on the steamers, like us. But your man, maybe, was sailin' foreign, an' made money? It's always a consuderation for a weedow."

"Not a penny," said the indiscreet Mrs MacCallum, as Para Handy wheeled her into a chair.

At eleven o'clock The Tar was missing. He had last been seen pulling off his new boots, which were too small for him, on the stair-head; and it was only after considerable searching the Captain and one of the Tarbert cousins found him sound asleep on the top of a chest in the neighbour's house.

"Colin," said the Captain, shaking him awake, "sit up and try and take something. See at the rest of us, as jovial as anything, and no' a man hit yet. Sit up and be smert for the credit of the *Fital Spark*."

"Are you angry wi' me, Captain?" asked The Tar.

"Not a bit of it, Colin! But you have the corkscrew in your pocket. I'm no' caring myself, but the Tarbert gentlemen will take it amiss. Forbye, there's your wife; you'll maybe have mind of her – wan Lucy MacCallum? She's in yonder, fine and cheery, wi' two of your Tarbert cousins holding her hand."

"Stop you! I'll hand them!" cried the exasperated bridegroom and bounded into the presence of the marriage-party in the house opposite, with a demonstration that finally led to the breaking-up of the party.

Next day took place The Tar's curious kirking. The MacCallums, as has been said, were not very regular churchgoers; in fact, they had overlooked the ordinances since the departed John died, and forgot that the church bell rang for the Sabbath-school an hour before it rang for the ordinary forenoon service.

Campbeltown itself witnessed the bewildering spectacle of The Tar and his bride followed by the mother and Para Handy, marching deliberately up the street and into the church among the children. Five minutes later they emerged, looking very red and ashamed of themselves.

"If I knew there wass so mich bother to mind things, I would never have got merried at all," said the bridegroom.

19

A STROKE OF LUCK

IT was a night of harmony on the good ship *Vital Spark*. She was fast in the mud at Colintraive quay, and, in the den of her, Para Handy was giving his song, "The Dancing Master" –

> "Set to Jeanie Mertin, tee-teedalum, tee-tadulam,
> Up the back and doon the muddle, tee-tadulam, tee-tadulam.
> Ye're wrong, Jeck, I'm certain; tee-tadulam, tee-tadulam,"

while the mate played an accompaniment on the trump – that is to say, the Jew's harp, a favourite instrument on steam-lighters where the melodeon has not intruded. The Captain knew only two verses, but he sang them over several times. "You're getting better and better at it every time," The Tar assured him, for The Tar had got the promise of a rise that day of a shilling a week on his pay. "If I had chust on my other boots," said the Captain, delighted at this appreciation. "This ones iss too light for singin' with –" and he stamped harder than ever as he went on with the song, for it was his idea that the singing of a song was a very ineffective and uninteresting performance unless you beat time with your foot on the floor.

The reason for the harmony on the vessel was that Dougie the mate had had a stroke of luck that evening. He had picked up at the quay-side a large and very coarse fish called a stenlock, or coal-fish, and had succeeded, by sheer effrontery, in passing it off as a cod worth two shillings on a guileless Glasgow woman who had come for the week to one of the Colintraive cottages.

"I'm only vexed I didna say it wass a salmon," said Dougie, when he came back to the vessel with his ill-got florin. "I could have got twice ass much for't."

"She would ken fine it wasna a salmon when it wasna in a tin," said the Captain.

"There's many a salmon that iss not in a canister," said the mate.

"Och ay, but she's from Gleska; they're awfu' Hielan' in Gleska aboot fush and things like that," said the Captain. "But it's maybe a peety you didn't say it wass a salmon, for two shullin's iss not mich among four of us."

"Among four of us!" repeated Dougie emphatically. "It's little enough among wan, let alone four; I'm going to keep her to mysel'."

"If that iss your opeenion, Dougie, you are maakin' a great mistake, and it'll maybe be better for you to shift your mind," the Captain said meaningly. "It iss the jyle you could be getting for swundling a poor cratur from Gleska that thinks a stenlock iss a cod. Forbye, it iss a tremendous risk, for you might be found oot, and it would be a disgrace to the *Fital Spark*."

Dougie was impressed by the possibility of trouble with the law as a result of his fish transaction, which, to do him justice, he had gone about more as a practical joke than anything else. "I'm vexed I did it, Peter," he said, turning the two shillings over in his hand. "I have a good mind to go up and tell the woman it wass chust a baur."

"Not at aal! not at aal!" cried Para Handy. "It wass a fine cod right enough; we'll chust send The Tar up to the Inn with the two shullin's and the jar, and we'll drink the Gleska woman's health that does not ken wan fish from another. It will be a lesson to her to be careful; chust that, to be careful."

So The Tar had gone to the Inn for the ale, and thus it was that harmony prevailed in the fo'c'sle of the *Vital Spark*.

"Iss that a song of your own doing?" asked Dougie, when the Captain was done.

"No," said Para Handy, "it iss a low-country song I heard wance in the Broomielaw. Yon iss the place for seeing life. I'm telling you it iss Gleska for gaiety if you have the money. There iss more life in wan day in the Broomielaw of Gleska than there iss in a fortnight on Loch Fyne."

"I daarsay there iss," said Dougie; "no' coontin' the herring."

"Och! life, life!" said the Captain, with a pensive air of ancient memory; "Gleska's the place for it. And the fellows iss there that iss not frightened, I'm telling you."

"I learned my tred there," mentioned the engineer, who had no accomplishments, and had not contributed anything to the evening's entertainment, and felt that it was time he was shining somehow.

"Iss that a fact, Macphail? I thocht it wass in a coal-ree in the country," said Para Handy. "I wass chust sayin', when Macphail put in his oar, that yon's the place for life. If I had my way of it, the *Fital Spark* would be going up every day to the Chamaica Brudge the same as the *Columba*, and I would be stepping ashore quite spruce with my Sunday clothes on, and no' lying here in a place like Colintraive, where there's no' even a polisman, with people that swundle a Gleska woman oot of only two shullin's. It wass not hardly worth your while, Dougie." The ale was now finished.

The mate contributed a reel and strathspey on the trump to the evening's programme, during which The Tar fell fast asleep, from which he wakened to suggest that he should give them a guess.

"Weel done, Colin!" said the Captain, who had never before seen such enterprise on the part of The Tar. "Tell us the guess if you can mind it."

"It begins something like this," said The Tar nervously: " 'Whether would you raither –' That's the start of it."

"Fine, Colin, fine!" said the Captain encouragingly.

"Take your breath and start again."

" 'Whether would you raither,' " proceeded The Tar – " 'whether would you raither or walk there?' "

"Say't again, slow," said Dougie, and The Tar repeated his extraordinary conundrum.

"If I had a piece of keelivine (lead pencil) and a lump of paper I could soon answer that guess," said the engineer, and the Captain laughed.

"Man Colin," he said, "you're missing half of the guess oot. There's no sense at aal in 'Whether would you raither or walk there?' "

"That's the way I heard it, anyway," said The Tar, sorry he had volunteered. " 'Whether would you raither or walk there?' I mind fine it wass that."

"Weel, we give it up anyway; what's the answer?" said the Captain.

"Man, I don't mind whether there wass an answer or no'," confessed The Tar, scratching his head; and the Captain irritably hit him with a cap on the ear, after which the entertainment terminated, and the crew of the *Vital Spark* went to bed.

Next forenoon a very irate-looking Glasgow woman was to be observed coming down the quay, and Dougie promptly retired into the hold of the *Vital Spark*, leaving the lady's reception to the Captain.

"Where's that man away to?" she asked Para Handy. "I want to speak to him."

"He's engaged, mem," said the Captain.

"I don't care if he's married," said the Glasgow woman; "I'm no' wantin' him. I jist wanted to say yon was a bonny-like cod he sell't me yesterday. I biled it three 'oors this mornin', and it was like leather when a' was done."

"That's droll," said the Captain. "It wass a fine fush, I'll assure you; if Dougie was here himsel' he would tell you. Maybe you didna boil it right. Cods iss curious that way. What did you use?"

"Watter!" snapped the Glasgow woman; "did you think I would use sand?"

"Chust that! chust that! Watter? Weel, you couldna use anything better for boilin' with than chust watter. What kind of coals did you use?"

"Jist plain black yins," said the woman. "I bocht them frae Cameron along the road there," referring to a coal agent who was a trade rival to the local charterer of the *Vital Spark*.

"Cameron!" cried Para Handy. "Wass I not sure there wass something or other wrong? Cameron's coals wouldna boil a wulk, let alone a fine cod. If Dougie wass here he would tell you that himsel'."

20

DOUGIE'S FAMILY

THE size of Dougie the mate's family might be considered a matter which was of importance to himself alone, but it was astonishing how much interest his shipmates took in it. When there was nothing else funny to talk about on the *Vital Spark*, they would turn their attention to the father of ten, and cunningly extract information from him about the frightful cost of boys' boots and the small measure of milk to be got for sixpence at Dwight's dairy in Plantation.

They would listen sympathetically, and later on roast him unmercifully with comments upon the domestic facts he had innocently revealed to them.

It might happen that the vessel would be lying at a West Highland quay, and the Captain sitting on deck reading a week-old newspaper, when he would wink at Macphail and The Tar, and say, "Cot bless me! boys, here's the price of boots goin' up; peety the poor faithers of big femilies." Or, "I see there's to be a new school started in Partick, Dougie; did you flit again?"

"You think you're smert, Peter," the mate would retort lugubriously. "Fun's fun, but I'll no' stand fun aboot my femily."

"Och! no offence, Dougald, no offence," Para Handy would say soothingly. "Hoo's the mustress keepin'?" and then ask a fill of tobacco to show his feelings were quite friendly.

In an ill-advised moment the parental pride and joy of the mate brought on board one day a cabinet photograph of himself and his wife and the ten children.

"What do you think of that?" he said to Para Handy, who took the extreme tip of one corner of the card between the finger and thumb of a hand black with coal-grime, glanced at the group, and said –

"Whatna Sunday School trup's this?"

"It's no' a trup at aal," said Dougie with annoyance.

"Beg pardon, beg pardon," said the Captain, "I see noo I wass wrong; it's Quarrier's Homes. Who's the chap wi' the whuskers in the muddle, that's greetin'?"

"Where's your eyes?" said Dougie. "It's no' a Homes at aal; that's me, and I'm no' greetin'. What would I greet for?"

"Faith, I believe you're right," said the Captain. "It's yoursel' plain enough, when I shut wan eye to look at it; but the collar and a clean face make a terrible dufference. Well, well, allooin' that it's you, and you're no greetin', it's rideeculous for you to be goin' to a dancin'-school."

"It's no' a dancin'-school, it's the femily," said the mate, losing his temper. "Fun's fun, but if you think I'll stand –"

"Keep caalm, keep caalm!" interrupted the Captain hurriedly, realising that he had carried the joke far enough. "I might have kent fine it wass the femily; they're aal ass like you both ass anything, and that'll be Susan the eldest."

"That!" said Dougie, quite mollified – "that's the mustress hersel'."

"Well, I'm jeegered," said the Captain, with well-acted amazement. "She's younger-looking than ever; that's a woman that's chust sublime."

The mate was so pleased he made him a present of the photograph.

But it always had been, and always would be, a distressing task to Dougie to have to intimate to the crew (as he had to do once a year) that there was a new addition to the family, for it was on these occasions that the chaff of his shipmates was most ingenious and galling. Only once, by a trick, had he got the better of them and evaded his annual roastings. On that occasion he

came to the *Vital Spark* with a black muffler on, and a sad countenance.

"I've lost my best freend," said he, rubbing his eyes to make them red.

"Holy smoke!" said Para Handy, "is Macmillan the pawnbroker deid?"

"It's no' him," said Dougie, manfully restraining a sob, and he went on to tell them that it was his favourite uncle, Jamie. He put so much pathos into his description of Uncle Jamie's last hours, that when he wound up by mentioning, in an off-hand way, that his worries were complicated by the arrival of another daughter that morning, the crew had, naturally, not the heart to say anything about it.

Some weeks afterwards they discovered by accident that he never had an Uncle Jamie.

"Man! he's cunning!" said Para Handy, when this black evidence of Dougie's astuteness came out. "Stop you till the next time, and we'll make him pay for it."

The suitable occasion for making the mate smart doubly for his deceit came in due course. Macphail the engineer lived in the next tenement to Dougie's family in Plantation, and he came down to the quay one morning before the mate, with the important intelligence for the Captain that the portrait group was now incomplete.

"Poor Dugald!" said the Captain sympathetically. "Iss it a child or a lassie?"

"I don't ken," said the engineer. "I just got a rumour frae the night polisman, and he said the wife was fine."

"Stop you and you'll see some fun with Dougie," said the Captain. "I'm mich mistaken if he'll swundle us this twict."

Para Handy had gone ashore for something, and was back before his mate appeared on board the *Vital Spark*, which was just starting for Campbeltown with a cargo of bricks. The mate took the wheel, smoked ceaselessly at a short cutty pipe, and said nothing; and nobody said anything to him.

"He's plannin' some other way oot of the scrape," whispered the Captain once to the engineer; "but he'll not get off so easy this time. Hold you on!"

It was dinner-time, and the captain, mate, and engineer were round the pot on deck aft, with The Tar at the wheel, within comfortable hearing distance, when Para Handy slyly broached the topic.

"Man, Dougie," he said, "what wass I doin' yonder last night but dreamin' in the Gaalic aboot you? I wass dreamin' you took a charter of the *Fital Spark* doon to Ardkinglas with a picnic, and there wass not a park in the place would hold the company."

Dougie simply grunted.

"It wass a droll dream," continued the Captain, diving for another potato. "I wass chust wonderin' hoo you found them aal at home. Hoo's the mustress keepin'?"

The mate got very red. "I wass chust goin' to tell you aboot her," he said with considerable embarrassment.

"A curious dream it wass," said Para Handy, postponing his pleasure, like the shrewd man he is, that he might enjoy it all the more when it came. "I saw you ass plain ass anything, and the *Fital Spark* crooded high and low with the picnic, and you in the muddle playing your trump. The mustress wass there, too, quite spruce, and – But you were goin' to say something aboot the mustress, Dougie. I hope she's in her usual?"

"That's chust it," said Dougie, more and more embarrassed as he saw his news had to be given now, if ever. "You would be thinkin' to yourself I wass late this mornin', but the fact iss we were in an aawful habble in oor hoose –"

"Bless me! I hope the lum didn't take fire nor nothing like that?" said Para Handy anxiously; and The Tar, at the wheel behind, was almost in a fit with suppressed laughter.

"Not at aal! worse nor that!" said Dougie in melancholy tones. "There's – there's – dash it! there's more boots than ever needed yonder!"

"Man, you're gettin' quite droll," said Para Handy. "Do you no' mind you told me aboot that wan chust three or four months ago?"

"You're a liar!" said Dougie, exasperated; "it's a twelvemonth since I told you aboot the last."

"Not at aal! not at aal! your mind's failin'," protested the Captain. "Five months ago at the most; you told me aboot it at the time. Surely there's some mistake?"

"No mistake at aal aboot it," said the mate, shaking his head so sadly that the Captain's heart was melted.

"Never mind, Dougald," he said, taking a little parcel out of his pocket. "I'm only in fun. I heard aboot it this mornin' from Macphail, and here's a wee bit peeny and a pair o' sluppers that I bought for't."

"To the muschief! It's no' an 'it'," said Dougie; "it's – it's – it's a twuns!"

"Holy smoke!" exclaimed Para Handy. "Iss that no chust desperate?" And the mate was so much moved that he left half his dinner and went forward towards the bow.

Para Handy went forward to him in a little and said, "Cheer up, Dougie; hoo wass I to ken it wass a twuns? If I had kent, it wouldna be the wan peeny and the wan sluppers; but I have two or three shillin's here, and I'll buy something else in Campbeltown."

"I can only – I can only say thankye the noo, Peter; it wass very good of you," said the mate, deeply touched, and attempting to shake the Captain's hand.

"Away! away!" said Para Handy, getting very red himself; "none of your chat! I'll buy peenies and sluppers if I like."

21

THE BAKER'S LITTLE WIDOW

O N the night after New Year's Day the Captain did a high-spirited thing he had done on the corresponding day for the previous six years; he had his hair cut and his beard trimmed by Dougie the mate, made a specially careful toilet – taking all the tar out of his hands by copious applications of salt butter – wound up his watch (which was never honoured in this way more than once or twice a twelvemonth), and went up the quay to propose to Mrs Crawford. It was one of the rare occasions upon which he wore a topcoat, and envied Macphail his Cairngorm scarfpin. There was little otherwise to suggest the ardent wooer, for ardent wooers do not look as solemn as Para Handy looked. The truth is he was becoming afraid that his persistency might wear down a heart of granite, and that this time the lady might accept him.

The crew of the *Vital Spark*, whom he thought quite ignorant of his tender passion for the baker's widow, took a secret but intense interest in this annual enterprise. He was supposed to be going to take tea with a cousin (as if captains took the tar off their hands to visit their own cousins!), and in order to make the deception more complete and allay any suspicions on the part, especially, of Macphail, who, as a great student of penny novelettes, was up to all the intrigues of love, the Captain casually mentioned that if it wasn't that it would vex his cousin he would sooner stay on the vessel and play Catch the Ten with them.

"I hate them tea-pairties," he said; "chust a way of wasting the New Year. But stay you here, boys, and I'll come back ass soon ass ever I can."

"Bring back some buns, or cookies, or buscuits wi' you," cried Dougie, as the Captain stepped on to the quay.

"What do you mean?" said Para Handy sharply, afraid he was discovered.

"Nothing, Peter, nothing at aal," the mate assured him, nudging The Tar in the dark. "Only it's likely you'll have more of them that you can eat at your cousin's tea-pairty."

Reassured thus that his secret was still safe, Para Handy went slowly up the quay. As he went he stopped a moment to exchange a genial word with everybody he met, as if time was of no importance, and he was only ashore for a daunder. This was because, dressed as he was, if he walked quickly and was not particularly civil to everybody, the whole of Campbeltown (which is a very observant place) would suspect he was up to something and watch him.

The widow's shop was at a conveniently quiet corner. He tacked back and forward off it in the darkness several times till a customer, who was being served, as he could see through the glass door, had come out, and a number of boys playing at "guesses" at the window had passed on, and then he cleared his throat, unbuttoned his topcoat and jacket to show his watch-chain, and slid as gently as he could in at the glass door.

"Dear me, fancy seeing you, Captain Macfarlane!" said the widow Crawford, coming from the room at the back of the shop. "Is it really yourself?"

"A good New Year to you," said the Captain, hurried and confused. "I wass chust goin' up the toon, and I thought I would give you a roar in the by-going. Are you keeping tip-top, Mery?"

His heart beat wildly; he looked at her sideways with a timid eye, for, hang it! she was more irresistible than ever. She was little, plump, smiling, rosy-cheeked, neat in dress, and just the exact age to make the Captain think he was young again.

"Will you not come ben and warm yourself? It's a nasty, damp night," said Mrs Crawford, pushing the back door, so that he got the most tempting vision of an interior with firelight dancing in it, a genial lamp, and a tea-table set.

"I'll chust sit doon and draw my breath for a meenute or two. You'll be busy?" said the Captain, rolling into the back room with an elephantine attempt (which she skilfully evaded) at playfully putting his arm round the widow's waist as he did so.

"You're as daft as ever, I see, Captain," said the lady. "I was just making myself a cup of tea; will you take one?"

"Och, it's puttin' you to bother," said the Captain.

"Not a bit of it," said the widow, and she whipped out a cup, which was suspiciously handy in a cupboard, and told the Captain to take off his coat and he would get the good of it when he went out.

People talk about young girls as entrancing. To men of experience like the Captain girls are insipid. The prime of life in the other sex is something under fifty; and the widow, briskly making tea, smiling on him, shaking her head at him, pushing him on the shoulder when he was impudent, chaffing him, surrounding him with an intoxicating atmosphere of homeliness, comfort, and cuddleability, seemed to Para Handy there and then the most angelic creature on earth. The rain could be heard falling heavily outside, no customers were coming in, and the back room of the baker's shop was, under the circumstances, as fine an earthly makeshift for Paradise as man could ask for.

Para Handy dived his hand into his coat pocket. "That minds me," said he; "I have a kind of a bottle of scent here a friend o' mine, by the name of Hurricane Jeck, took home for me from America last week. It's the rale Florida Water; no' the like o't to be got here, and if you put the least sensation on your hanky you'll feel the smell of it a mile away. It's chust sublime."

"Oh! it's so kind of you!" said the widow, beaming on him with the merriest, brownest, deepest, meltingest of eyes, and letting her plump little fingers linger a moment on his as she took the perfume bottle. The Captain felt as if golden harps were singing in the air, and fairies were tickling him down the back with peacocks' feathers.

"Mery," he said in a little, "this iss splendid tea. Capital, aalthegither!"

"Tuts! Captain," said she, "is it only my tea you come to pay compliments to once a year? Good tea's common enough if you're willing to pay for it. What do you think of myself?"

The Captain neatly edged his chair round the corner of the table to get it close beside hers, and she just as neatly edged her chair round the other corner, leaving their relative positions exactly as they had been.

"No, no, Captain," said she, twinkling; "hands off the widow. I'm a done old woman, and it's very good of you to come and have tea with me; but I always thought sailors, with a sweetheart, as they say, in every port, could say nice things to cheer up a lonely female heart. What we women need, Captain – the real necessity of our lives – is some one to love us. Even if he's at the other end of the world, and unlikely ever to be any nearer, it makes the work of the day cheery. But what am I haverin' about?" she added, with a delicious, cosy, melting, musical sigh that bewitchingly heaved her blouse. "Nobody cares for me, I'm too old."

"Too old!" exclaimed the Captain, amused at the very idea. "You're not a day over fifty. You're chust sublime."

"Forty-nine past, to be particular," said the widow, "and feel like twenty. Oh! Captain, Captain! you men!"

"Mery," entreated Para Handy, putting his head to one side, "caal me Peter, and gie me a haad o' your hand." This time he edged his chair round quicker than she did hers, and captured her fingers. Now that he had them he didn't know very well what to do with them, but he decided after a little that a cute thing to do was to pull them one by one and try to make them crack. He did so, and got slapped on the ear for his pains.

"What do you mean by that?" said she.

"Och, it was chust a baur, Mery," said Para Handy. "Man, you're strong, strong! You would make a sublime wife for any sober, decent, good-looking, capable man. You would make a fine wife for a sailor, and I'm naming no names, mind ye; but" here he winked in a manner that seemed to obliterate one complete side of his face – "they caal him Peter. Eh? What?"

"Nobody would have me," said the widow, quite cheerfully, enjoying herself immensely. "I'm old – well, kind of old, and plain, and I have no money."

"Money!" said Para Handy contemptuously; "the man I'm thinking of does not give wan docken for money. And you're no more old than I am mysel', and as for bein' plain, chust look at the lovely polka you have on and the rudness of your face. If Dougie was here he would tell – no, no, don't mention a cheep to Dougie – not a cheep; he would maybe jalouse something."

"This is the sixth time of asking, Captain," said the widow. "You must have your mind dreadful firm made up. But it's only at the New Year I see you; I'm afraid you're like all sailors – when you're away you forget all about me. Stretch your hand and have another London bun."

"London buns iss no cure for my case," said the Captain, taking one, however. "I hope you'll say yes this time."

"I'll – I'll think about it," said the widow, still smiling; "and if you're passing this way next New Year and call in, I'll let you know."

The crew of the *Vital Spark* waited on deck for the return of the skipper. Long before he came in sight they heard him clamping down the quay singing cheerfully to himself –

"Rolling home to bonnie Scotland,
    Rolling home, dear land, to thee;
Rolling home to bonnie Scotland,
    Rolling home across the sea."

"Iss your cousin's tea-pairty over already?" said Dougie innocently. "Wass there many at it?"

"Seven or eight," said Para Handy promptly. "I chust came away. And I'm feeling chust sublime. Wan of Brutain's hardy sons."

He went down below, and hung up his topcoat and his watch and took off his collar, which uncomfortably rasped his neck. "Mery's the right sort," said he to himself; "she's no' going ram-stam into the business. She's caautious like mysel'. Maybe next New Year she'll make her mind up."

And the widow, putting up her shutters that night, hummed cheerfully to herself, and looked quite happy. "I wish I HAD called him Peter," she thought; "next year I'll not be so blate."

22

THREE DRY DAYS

ON the first day of February the Captain of the *Vital Spark* made an amazing resolution. Life in the leisure hours of himself and his crew had been rather strenuous during the whole of January, for Dougie had broken the Rechabites. When Dougie was not a Rechabite, he always carried about with him an infectious atmosphere of gaiety and a half-crown, and the whole ship's company took its tone from him. This is a great moral lesson. It shows how powerful for good or evil is the influence and example of One Strong Man. If Dougie had been more at home that month, instead of trading up the West Coast, his wife would have easily dispelled his spirit of gaiety by making him nurse the twins, and she would have taken him herself to be reinstalled in the Rechabites, for she was "a fine, smert, managin' woman", as he admitted himself; but when sailors are so often and so far away from the benign influences of home, with nobody to search their pockets, it is little wonder they should sometimes be foolish.

So the Captain rose on the first day of the month with a frightful headache, and emphatically refused to adopt the customary method of curing it. "No," he said to his astonished mates, "I'm no' goin' up to the Ferry Hoose nor anywhere else; I'm teetotal."

"Teetotal!" exclaimed Dougie, much shocked. "You shouldna make a joke aboot things like that, and you no' feelin' very weel; come on up and take your mornin'."

"Not a drop!" said Para Handy firmly.

"Tut, tut, Peter; chust wan beer," persisted the mate patiently.

"Not even if it wass jampaigne," said the Captain, drying his head, which he had been treating to a cold douche. "My mind's made up. Drink's a curse, and I'm done wi't, for I canna stand it."

"There's nobody askin' you to stand it," explained the mate. "I have a half-croon o' my own here."

"It's no odds," said the Captain. "I'm on the teetotal tack. Not another drop will I taste –"

"Stop, stop!" interrupted Dougie, more shocked than ever. "Don't do anything rash. You might be struck doon deid, and then you would be sorry for what you said. Do you mean to tell us that you're goin' to be teetotal aalthegither?"

"No," said the Captain, "I'm no' that desperate. I wouldna care chust to go aal that length, but I'm goin' to be teetotal for the month o' February."

"Man, I think you're daft, Peter," said the mate. "February, of aal months! In February the New Year's no' right bye, and the Gleska Fair's chust comin' on; could you no' put it off for a more sensible time?"

"No," said the Captain firmly, "February's the month for me; there's two or three days less in't than any other month in the year."

So the crew filed ashore almost speechless with astonishment – annoyed and depressed to some extent by this inflexible virtue on the part of Para Handy.

"He's gettin' quite droll in his old age," was Dougie's explanation.

"Fancy him goin' away and spoilin' the fun like that!" said The Tar incredulously.

"I aye said he hadna the game in him," was the comment of Macphail the engineer.

Para Handy watched them going up to the Ferry House, and wished it was the month of March.

The first day of his abstinence would have passed without much more inclination on his part to repent his new resolution were it not for the fact that half a score of circumstances conspired to make it a day of unusual trial. He met friends that day he had not met for months, all with plenty of time on their hands; Hurricane Jack, the irresistible, came alongside in another vessel, and was immediately for celebrating this coincidence by having half a day off, a proposal the Captain evaded for a while only by pretending to be seriously ill and under medical treatment; the coal merchant, whose cargo they had just discharged, presented the crew with a bottle of whisky; there was a ball at the George Hotel; there was a travelling piper on the streets, with most inspiring melodies; the headache was away by noon – only a giant will-power could resist so many circumstances conducive to gaiety. But Para Handy never swerved in his resolution. He compromised with the friends who had plenty of time and the inclination for merriment by taking fills of tobacco from them; confiscated the bottle of whisky as Captain, and locked it past with the assurance to his crew that it would be very much the more matured if kept till March; and the second time Hurricane Jack came along the quay to see if the Captain of the *Vital Spark* was not better yet, he accompanied him to the Ferry House, and startled him by saying he would have "Wan small half of lime-juice on draught".

"What's that, Peter?" said Hurricane Jack. "Did I hear you say something aboot lime-juice, or does my ears deceive me?"

"It's chust for a bate, Jeck – no offence," explained the Captain hurriedly. "I have a bate on wi' a chap that I'll no' drink anything stronger this month; but och! next month, if we're spared, wait you and you'll see some fine fun."

Hurricane Jack looked at him with great disapproval. "Macfarlane," he said solemnly, "you're goin' far, far wrong, and mind you I'm watchin' you. A gembler iss an abomination, and gemblin' at the expense of your inside iss worse than gemblin' on horses. Us workin' men have nothing but oor strength to go on, and if we do not keep up oor strength noo and then, where are we? You will chust have a smaal gill, and the man that made the bate wi' you'll never be any the wiser."

"No, Jeck, thank you aal the same," said the Captain, "but I'll chust take the lime-juice. Where'll you be on the first o' Merch?"

Hurricane Jack grudgingly ordered the lime-juice, and asked the landlady to give the Captain a sweetie with it to put away the taste, then looked on with an aspect of mingled incredulity and disgust as Para Handy hurriedly gulped the unaccustomed beverage and chased it down with a drink of water.

"It's a fine thing a drap watter," said Para Handy, gasping.

"No' a worse thing you could drink," said Hurricane Jack. "It rots your boots; what'll it no' do on your inside? Watter's fine for sailin' on – there's nothing better – but it's no' drink for sailors."

On the second day of the great reform Para Handy spent his leisure hours fishing for saithe from the side of the vessel, and was, to all appearance, firmer than ever. He was threatened for a while by a good deal of interference from his crew, who resented the confiscation of the presentation bottle, but he turned the tables on them by coming out in the *rôle* of temperance lecturer. When they approached him, he sniffed suspiciously, and stared at their faces in a way that was simply galling – to Dougie particularly, who was naturally of a rubicund countenance. Then he sighed deeply, shook his head solemnly, and put on a fresh bait.

"Are you no' better yet?" Dougie asked. "You're looking ass dull ass if the shup wass tied up to a heidstone in the Necropolis o' Gleska. None o' your didoes, Peter; give us oot the spurits we got the present o'. It's Candlemas."

Para Handy stared at his fishing-line, and said gently, as if he were speaking to himself, "Poor sowls! poor sowls! Nothing in their heids but drink. It wass a happy day for me the day I gave it up, or I might be like the rest o' them. There's poor Dougald lettin' it get a terrible grup o' him; and The Tar chust driftin', driftin' to the poor's-hoose, and Macphail iss sure to be in the horrors before Setturday, for he hasna the heid for drink, him no' bein' right Hielan'."

"Don't be rash; don't do anything you would be vexed for, but come on away up the toon and have a pant," said Dougie coaxingly. "Man, you have only to make up your mind and shake it off, and you'll be ass cheery ass ever you were."

"He's chust takin' a rise oot o' us; are you no', Captain?" said The Tar, anxious to leave his commander an honourable way of retreat from his preposterous position.

Para Handy went on fishing as if they were not present.

"Merried men, too, with wifes and femilies," he said musingly. "If they chust knew what it wass, like me, to be risin' in the mornin' wi' a clear heid, and a good conscience, they would never touch it again. I never knew what happiness wass till I joined the teetotal, and it'll be money in my pocket forbye."

"You'll go on, and you'll go on with them expuriments too far till you'll be a vegetarian next," said Dougie, turning away. "Chust a vegetarian, tryin' to live on turnips and gress, the same ass a coo. If I was a Macfarlane I wouldna care to be a coo."

Then they left him with an aspect more of sorrow than of anger, and he went on fishing.

The third day of the month was Saturday; there was nothing to do on the *Vital Spark*, which was waiting on a cargo of timber, so all the crew except the Captain spent the time ashore. Him they left severely alone, and the joys of fishing saithe and reading a week-old newspaper palled.

"The worst of bein' good iss that it leaves you duvvelish lonely," said the Captain to himself.

An hour later, he discovered that he had a touch of toothache, and, strongly inclined for a temporary suspension of the new rules for February, he went to the locker for the presentation bottle.

It was gone!

23

THE VALENTINE THAT MISSED FIRE

A FORTNIGHT of strict teetotalism on the part of the Captain was too much of a joke for his crew. "It's just bounce," said the mate; "he's showin' off. I'm a Rechabite for six years, every time I'm in Gleska; but I never let it put between me and a gless of good Brutish spurits wi' a shipmate in any port, Loch Fyne or foreign."

"It's most annoyin'," said The Tar. "He asked me yesterday if my health wassna breakin' doon wi' drink, the same ass it would break doon wi' aal I take."

"Chust what I told you; nothing but bounce!" said Dougie gloomily. "Stop you! Next time he's in trum, I'll no' be so handy at pullin' corks for him. If I wass losin' my temper wi' him, I would give him a bit o' my mind."

The engineer, wiping his brow with a wad of oily waste, put down the penny novelette he was reading and gave a contemptuous snort. "I wonder to hear the two o' ye talkin'," said he. "Ye're baith feared for him. I could soon fix him."

"Could you, Macphail?" said Dougie. "You're aawful game: what would you do?"

"I would send him a valentine that would vex him," replied the engineer promptly; "a fizzer o' a valentine that would mak' his hair curl for him."

The mate impulsively smacked his thigh. "My Chove! Macphail," said he, "it's the very ticket! What do you say to a valentine for the Captain, Colin?"

"Whatever you think yersel'," said The Tar.

That night Dougie and The Tar went ashore at Tarbert for a valentine. There was one shop-window up the town with a gorgeous display of penny "mocks", designed and composed to give the recipient in every instance a dull, sickening thud on the bump of his self-esteem. The two mariners saw no valentine, however, that quite met the Captain's case.

"There'll be plenty o' other wans inside on the coonter," said Dougie diplomatically. "Away you in, Colin, and pick wan suitable, and I'll stand here and watch."

"Watch what?" inquired The Tar suspiciously. "It would be more like the thing if you went in and bought it yoursel'; I'll maybe no' get wan that'll please you."

"Aal you need to ask for iss a mock valentine, lerge size, and pretty broad, for a skipper wi' big feet. I would go in mysel' in a meenute if it wassna that – if it wassna that it would look droll, and me a muddle-aged man wi' whuskers."

The Tar went into the shop reluctantly, and was horrified to find a rather pretty girl behind the counter. He couldn't for his life suggest mock valentines to her, and he could not with decency back out without explanation.

"Have you any – have you any nice unvelopes?" he inquired bashfully, as she stood waiting his order.

"What size?" she asked.

"Lerge size, and pretty broad, for a skipper wi' big feet," said The Tar in his confusion. Then he corrected himself, adding, "Any size, muss, suitable for holdin' letters."

"There's a great run on that kind of envelope this winter," the lady remarked, being a humorist. "How many?"

"A ha'pennyworth," said The Tar. "I'll chust take them wi' me."

When The Tar came out of the shop the mate was invisible, and it was only after some search he found him in a neighbouring public-house.

"I chust came in here to put by the time," said Dougie; "but seein' you're here, what am I for?"

The Tar, realising that there must be an unpleasant revelation immediately, produced the essential threepence and paid for beer.

"I hope you got yon?" said the mate anxiously.

"Ass sure ass daith, Dougie, I didna like to ask for it," explained the young man pathetically. "There's a gasalier and two paraffin lamps bleezin' in the shop, and it would gie me a rud face to ask for a mock valentine in such an illumination. Iss there no other wee dark shop in the toon we could get what we want in?"

The mate surveyed him with a disgusted countenance. "Man, you're a coward, Colin," he said. "The best in the land goes in and buys mock valentines, and it's no disgrace to nobody so long ass he has the money in his hand. If I had another gless o' beer I would go in mysel'."

"You'll get that!" said The Tar gladly, and produced another threepence, after which they returned to the shop-window, where Dougie's courage apparently failed him, in spite of the extra glass of beer. "It's no' that I give a docken for anybody," he explained, "but you see I'm that weel kent in Tarbert. What sort o' body keeps the shop?"

"Ooh, it's chust an old done man wi' a sore hand and wan eye no' neebours," replied The Tar strategically. "Ye needna be frightened for him; he'll no' say a cheep. To bleezes wi' him!"

Dougie was greatly relieved at this intelligence. "Toots!" he said. "Iss that aal? Watch me!" and he went banging in at the door in three strides.

The lady of the shop was in a room behind. To call her attention Dougie cried, "Shop!" and kicked the front of the counter, with his eyes already on a pile of valentines ready for a rush of business in that elegant form of billet-doux. When the pretty girl came skipping out of the back room, he was even more astounded and alarmed than The Tar had been.

"A fine night," he remarked affably: "iss your faither at the back?"

"I think you must have made a mistake in the shop," said the lady. "Who do you want?"

"Him with the sore hand and the wan eye no' right neebours," said the mate, not for a moment suspecting that The Tar had misled him. "It's parteecular business; I'll no' keep him wan meenute."

"There's nobody here but myself," the girl informed him, and then he saw he had been deceived by his shipmate.

"Stop you till I get that Tar!" he exclaimed with natural exasperation, and was on the point of leaving when the pile of valentines met his eye again, and he decided to brazen it out.

"Maybe you'll do yoursel'," said he, with an insinuating leer at the shopkeeper. "There iss a shipmate o' mine standin' oot there took a kind o' notion o' a mock valentine and doesna like to ask for't. He wass in a meenute or two ago – you would know him by the warts on his hand – but he hadna the nerve to ask for it."

"There you are, all kinds," said the lady, indicating the pile on the counter, with a smile of comprehension. "A penny each."

Dougie wet his thumb and clumsily turned over the valentines, seeking for one appropriate to a sea captain silly enough to be teetotal. "It's chust for a baur, mind you," he explained to the lady. "No herm at aal, at aal; chust a bit of a high jeenk. Forbye, it's no' for me: it's for the other fellow, and his name's Colin Turner, but he's blate, blate." He raised his voice so that The Tar, standing outside the window, could hear him quite plainly; with the result that The Tar was so ashamed, he pulled down his cap on his face and hurriedly walked off to the quay.

"There's an awful lot o' them valentines for governesses and tylers and polismen," said Dougie; "the merchant service doesna get mich of a chance. Have you nothing smert and nippy that'll fit a sea captain, and him teetotal?"

The shopkeeper hurriedly went over her stock, and discovered that teetotalism was the one eccentricity valentines never dealt with; on the contrary, they were all for people with red noses and bibulous propensities.

"There's none for teetotal captains," said she; "but here's one for a captain that's not teetotal," and she shoved a valentine with a most unpleasant-looking seaman, in a state of intoxication, walking arm-in-arm with a respectable-looking young woman.

"Man, that's the very tup!" said Dougie, delighted. "It's ass clever a thing ass ever I seen. I wonder the way they can put them valentines thegither. Read what it says below, I havena my specs."

The shopkeeper read the verse on the valentine:

"The girl that would marry a man like you
Would have all the rest of her life to rue;
A sailor soaked in salt water and rum
Could never provide a happy home."

"Capital!" exclaimed the mate, highly delighted. "Ass smert ass anything in the works of Burns. That wan'll do splendid."

"I thought it was for a teetotal captain you wanted one," said the lady, as she folded up the valentine.

"He's only teetotal to spite us," said Dougie. "And that valentine fits him fine, for he's coortin' a baker's weedow, and he thinks we don't know. Mind you, it's no' me that's goin' to send the valentine, it's Colin Turner; but there's no herm, chust a bit of a baur. You ken yoursel'."

Then an embarrassing idea occurred to him – Who was to address the envelope?

"Do you keep mournin' unvelopes?" he asked.

"Black-edged envelopes – yes," said the shopkeeper.

"Wan," said Dougie; and when he got it he put the valentine inside and ventured to propose to the lady that, seeing she had pen and ink handy, she might address the envelope for him, otherwise the recipient would recognise Colin Turner's hand-of-write.

The lady obliged, and addressed the document to

CAPTAIN PETER MACFARLANE,

SS. VITAL SPARK,

TARBERT.

Dougie thanked her effusively on behalf of The Tar, paid for his purchases and a penny stamp, and went out. As he found his shipmate gone, he sealed the envelope and posted it.

When the letter-carrier came down Tarbert quay next morning, all the crew of the *Vital Spark* were on deck – the Captain in blissful unconsciousness of what was in store for him, the others anxious not to lose the expression of his countenance when he should open his valentine.

It was a busy day on the *Vital Spark*; all hands had to help to get in a cargo of wood.

"A mournin' letter for you, Captain," said the letter-carrier, handing down the missive.

Para Handy looked startled, and walked aft to open it. He took one short but sufficient glimpse at the valentine, with a suspicious glance at the crew, who were apparently engrossed in admiration of the scenery round Tarbert. Then he went down the fo'c'sle, to come up a quarter of an hour later with his good clothes on, his hat, and a black tie.

"What the duvvle game iss he up to noo?" said Dougie, greatly astonished.

"I hope it didna turn his brain," said The Tar. "A fright sometimes does it. Wass it a very wild valentine, Dougie?"

Para Handy moved aft with a sad, resigned aspect, the mourning envelope in his hand. "I'm sorry I'll have to go away till the efternoon, boys," he said softly. "See and get in that wud nice and smert before I come back."

"What's wrong?" asked Dougie, mystified.

The Captain ostentatiously blew his nose, and explained that they might have noticed he had just got a mourning letter.

"Was't a mournin' wan? I never noticed," said Dougie.

"Neither did I," added The Tar hurriedly.

"Yes," said the Captain sadly, showing them the envelope; "my poor cousin Cherlie over in Dunmore iss no more; he just slipped away yesterday, and I'm goin' to take the day off and make arrangements."

"Well, I'm jiggered!" exclaimed Dougie, as they watched Para Handy walking off on what they realised was to be a nice holiday at their expense, for they would now have his share of the day's work to do as well as their own.

"Did ye ever see such a nate liar?" said The Tar, lost in admiration at the cunning of the Captain.

And then they fell upon the engineer, and abused him for suggesting the valentine.

24

THE DISAPPOINTMENT OF ERCHIE'S NIECE

PARA HANDY never had been at a Glasgow ball till he went to the Knapdale Natives', and he went there simply to please Hurricane Jack. That gallant and dashing mariner came to him one day at Bowling, treated him to three substantial refreshments in an incredibly short space of time, and then delivered a brilliant lecture on the duty of being patriotic to one's native place, "backing up the boys", and buying a ticket for the assembly in question.

"But I'm not a native of Knapdale," said the Captain. "Forbye, I'm kind of oot o' the dancin'; except La Va and Petronella I don't mind wan step."

"That's aal right, Peter," said Hurricane Jack encouragingly; "there's nobody'll make you dance at a Knapdale ball if you're no' in trum for dancin'. I can get you on the committee, and aal you'll have to do will be to stand at the door of the committee room and keep the crood back from the beer-bottles. I'm no' there mysel' for amusement: do you ken Jean Mactaggart?"

"Not me," said Para Handy. "What Mactaggarts iss she off, Jeck?"

"Carradale," said Hurricane Jack modestly. "A perfect beauty! We're engaged."

The Captain shook hands mournfully with his friend and cheerlessly congratulated him. "It's a responsibility, Jeck," he said, "there's no doot it's a responsibility, but you ken yoursel' best."

"She's a nice enough gyurl so far ass I know," said Hurricane Jack. "Her brother's in the

Western Ocean tred. What I'm wantin' you on the committee for iss to keep me back from the committee room, so that I'll not take a drop too much and affront the lassie. If you see me desperate keen on takin' more than would be dacent, take a dozen strong smert fellows in wi' you at my expense and barricade the door. I'll maybe taalk aboot tearin' the hoose doon, but och, that'll only be my nonsense."

The Captain accepted the office, not without reluctance, and went to the ball, but Hurricane Jack failed to put in any appearance all night, and Para Handy considered himself the victim of a very stupid practical joke on the part of his friend.

Early next forenoon Hurricane Jack presented himself on board the *Vital Spark* and made an explanation. "I'm black affronted, Peter," he said, "but I couldna help it. I had a bit of an accident. You see it wass this way, Peter. Miss Mactaggart wass comin' special up from Carradale and stayin' with her uncle, old Macpherson. She wass to put her clothes on there, and I wass to caal for her in wan of them cabs at seven o'clock. I wass ready at five, all spruce from clew to earing, and my heid wass that sore wi' wearin' a hat for baals that I got hold of a couple of men I knew in the China tred and went for chust wan small wee gless. What happened efter that for an 'oor or two's a mystery, but I think I wass drugged. When I got my senses I wass in a cab, and the driver roarin' doon the hatch to me askin' the address.

"'What street iss it you're for?' said he.

"'What streets have you?' I asked.

"'Aal you told me wass Macfarlane's shup,' he said; 'do you think we're anyway near it?'

"When he said that I put my heid oot by the gless and took an observation.

"'Iss this Carrick Street or Monday mornin'?' says I to him, and then he put me oot of his cab. The poor sowl had no fear in him; he must have been Irish. It wass not much of a cab; here's the door handles, a piece of the wud, and the man's brass number; I chust took them with me for identification, and went home to my bed. When I wakened this mornin' and thought of Jean sittin' up aal night waitin' on me, I wass clean demented."

"It's a kind of a peety, too, the way it happened," said Para Handy sympathetically. "It would put herself a bit aboot sittin' aal night wi' her sluppers on."

"And a full set o' new sails," said Hurricane Jack pathetically. "She was sparin' no expense. This'll be a lesson to me. It'll do me good; I wish it hadna happened. What I called for wass to see if you'll be kind enough, seein' you were on the committee, to go up to 191 Barr Street, where she's stayin' wi' Macpherson, and put the thing ass nicely for me ass you can."

Para Handy was naturally shy of the proposal. "I never saw the lassie," said he. "Would it no' look droll for me to go instead of yoursel'?"

"It would look droll if you didna," said Hurricane Jack emphatically. "What are you on the committee for, and in cherge of aal the beer, unless you're to explain things? I'll show you the close, and you'll go up and ask for two meenutes' private conversation with Miss Mactaggart, and you'll tell her that I'm far from weel. Say I wass on my way up last night in fine time and the cab collided with a tramway car. Break it nice, and no' frighten the poor gyurl oot of her senses. Say I was oot of my conscience for seven 'oors, but that I'm gettin' the turn, and I'm no' a bit disfigured."

Para Handy was still irresolute. "She'll maybe want to nurse you, the way they do in Macphail's novelles," said he, "and what'll I tell her then?"

This was a staggerer for Hurricane Jack. He recognised the danger of arousing the womanly sympathies of Miss Mactaggart. But he was equal to all difficulties of this kind. "Tell her," said he, "there's nobody to get speakin' to me for forty-eight 'oors, but that I'll likely be oot on Monday."

The Captain agreed to undertake this delicate mission, but only on condition that Dougie the mate should accompany him to back him up in case his own resourcefulness as a liar should fail him at the critical moment.

"Very well," said Hurricane Jack, "take Dougie wi' you, but watch her uncle; I'm told he's cunning, cunning, though I never met him – a man Macpherson, by the name of Erchie. Whatever you tell her, if he's there at the time, tell it to her in the Gaalic."

Para Handy and his mate that evening left Hurricane Jack at a discreet public bar called the "Hot Blast", and went up to the house of Erchie Macpherson. It was himself who came to answer their knock at his door, for he was alone in the house.

"We're no' for ony strings o' onions, or parrots, or onything o' that sort," he said, keeping one foot against the door and peering at them in the dim light of the rat-tail burner on the stair-landing. "And if it's the stair windows ye want to clean, they were done yesterday."

"You should buy specs," said the Captain promptly – "they're no' that dear. Iss Miss Mactaggart in?"

Erchie opened the door widely, and gave his visitors admission to the kitchen.

"She's no' in the noo," said he. "Which o' ye happens to be the sailor chap that was to tak' her to the ball last nicht?"

"It wasna any o' us," said Para Handy. "It wass another gentleman aalthegither."

"I micht hae kent that," said Erchie. "Whit lockup is he in? If it's his bail ye're here for, ye needna bother. I aye tell't my guid-sister's dochter she wasna ill to please when she took up wi' a sailor. I had a son that was yince a sailor himsel', but thank the Lord he's better, and he's in the Corporation noo. Were ye wantin' to see Jean?"

"Chust for a meenute," said Para Handy, quietly taking a seat on the jawbox. "Will she be long?"

"Five feet three," said Erchie, "and broad in proportion. She hasna come doon sae much as ye wad think at her disappointment."

"That's nice," said Para Handy. "A thing o' the kind would tell terribly on some weemen. You're no' in the shuppin' tred yoursel', I suppose? I ken a lot o' Macphersons in the coast line. But I'm no' askin', mind ye; it's chust for conversation. There wass a femily of Macphersons came from the same place ass mysel' on Lochfyne-side; fine smert fellows they were, but I daresay no relation. Most respectable. Perhaps you ken the Gaalic?"

"Not me!" said Erchie frankly – "jist plain Gleska. If I'm Hielan' I canna help it; my faither took the boat to the Broomielaw as soon as he got his senses."

The conversation would have languished here if Dougie had not come to the rescue. "What's your tred?" he asked bluntly.

"Whiles I beadle and whiles I wait," replied Erchie, who was not the man to be ashamed of his calling. "At ither times I jist mind my ain affairs; ye should gie 't a trial – it'll no hurt ye."

The seamen laughed at this sally: it was always a virtue of both of them that they could appreciate a joke at their own expense.

"No offence, no offence, Mr Macpherson," said Para Handy. "I wish your niece would look slippy. You'll be sorry to hear aboot what happened to poor Jeck."

Erchie turned quite serious. "What's the maitter wi' him?" he said.

"The cab broke doon last night," said the Captain solemnly, "and he got a duvvle of a smash."

"Puir sowl!" said Erchie, honestly distressed. "This'll be a sair blow for Jeanie."

"He lost his conscience for 'oors, but there's no disfeegurement, and he'll be speechless till Monday mornin'. It's a great peety. Such a splendid voice ass he had, too; it wass truly sublime. He's lyin' yonder wi' his heid in a sling and not wan word in him. He tell't me I was to say to –"

Here Dougie, seeing an inconsistency in the report, slyly nudged his captain, who stopped short and made a very good effort at a sigh of deep regret.

"I thocht ye said he couldna speak," said Erchie suspiciously.

"My mistake, my mistake," said the Captain. "What I meant wass that he could only speak in the Gaalic; the man's fair off his usual. Dougie'll tell you himsel'."

Dougie shook his head lugubriously. "Ay," said he, "he's yonder wi' fifteen doctors roond him waitin' for the turn."

"What time did it happen?" inquired Erchie. "Was it efter he was here?"

"He wass on his way here," said Para Handy. "It was exactly half-past seven, for his watch stopped in the smash."

At this Erchie sat back in his chair and gave a disconcerting laugh. "Man," he said, "ye're no' bad at a baur, but ye've baith put yer feet in't this time. Will ye tak' a refreshment? There's a drop speerits in the hoose and a bottle or two o' porter."

"I'm teetotal mysel' at present," said Para Handy, "but I have a nesty cold. I'll chust take the spurits while you're pullin' the porter. We'll drink a quick recovery to Jeck."

"Wi' a' my he'rt," said Erchie agreeably. "I hope he'll be oot again afore Monday. Do ye no' ken he came here last nicht wi' the cab a' richt, but was that dazed Jeanie wadna gang wi' him. But she got to the ball a' the same, for she went wi' Mackay the polisman."

"My Chove!" said the Captain, quite dumbfoundered. "He doesna mind, himself, a thing aboot it."

"I daresay no'," said Erchie, "that's the warst o' trevellin' in cabs; he should hae come in a motor-caur."

When the Captain and Dougie came down Macpherson's stair, they considered the situation in the close.

"I think mysel'," said the Captain, "it wouldna be salubrious for neither o' the two of us to go to the, 'Hot Blast' and break the news to Jeck the night."

"Whatever ye think yoursel'," said Dougie, and they headed straight for home.

25

PARA HANDY'S WEDDING

I T is possible that Para Handy might still have been a bachelor if Calum Cameron had not been jilted. Three days before Calum was to have been married, the girl exercised a girl's privilege and changed her mind. She explained her sad inconstancy by saying she had never cared for him, and only said "yes" to get him off her face. It was an awkward business, because it left the baker's widow, Mrs Crawford, with a large bride's-cake on her hands. It is true the bride's-cake had been paid for, but in the painful circumstances neither of the parties to the broken contract would have anything to do with it, and it continued to lie in the baker's window, a pathetic evidence of woman's perfidy. All Campbeltown talked about it; people came five and six miles in from the country to look at it. When they saw what a handsome example of the confectioner's art it was, they shook their heads and said the lassie could have no heart, let alone good taste.

Mrs Crawford, being a smart business woman, put a bill in the window with the legend –

EXCELLENT BRIDE'S-CAKE

SECOND-HAND

17/6

But there were no offers, and she was on the point of disposing of it on the Art Union principle, when, by one of those providential accidents that are very hard on the sufferer but lead by a myriad consequent circumstances to the most beneficent ends, a man in Carrick Street, Glasgow, broke his leg. The man never heard of Para Handy in all his life, nor of the *Vital Spark*; he had never been in Campbeltown, and if he had not kept a pet tortoise he would never have figured in this book, and Para Handy might not have been married, even though Calum Cameron's girl had been a jilt.

The Carrick Street man's tortoise had wandered out into the close in the evening; the owner, rushing out hurriedly at three minutes to ten to do some shopping, tripped over it, and was not prevented by the agony of his injured limb from seizing the offending animal and throwing it into the street, where it fell at the feet of Para Handy, who was passing at the time.

"A tortoise!" said the Captain, picking it up. "The first time ever I kent they flew. I'll take it to Macphail – he's keen on birds anyway," and down he took it to the engineer of the *Vital Spark*.

But Macphail refused to interest himself in a pet which commended itself neither by beauty of plumage nor sweetness of song, and for several days the unhappy tortoise took a deck passage on the *Vital Spark*, its constitution apparently little impaired by the fact that at times The Tar used it as a coal-hammer.

"I'll no' see the poor tortoise abused this way," said Para Handy, when they got to Campbeltown one day; "I'll take it up and give it to a friend o' mine," and, putting it into his pocket in the evening, he went up to the baker's shop.

The widow was at the moment fixing a card on the bride's-cake intimating that tickets for the raffle of it would cost sixpence each, and that the drawing would take place on the following Saturday. Her plump form was revealed in the small shop-window; the flush of exertion charmingly irradiated her countenance as she bent among her penny buns and bottles of fancy biscuits; Para Handy, gazing at her from the outside, thought he had never seen her look more attractive. She blushed more deeply when she saw him looking in at her, and retired from the window with some embarrassment as he entered the shop.

"Fine night, Mery," said the Captain. "You're pushin' business desperate, surely, when you're raffling bride's-cakes."

"Will you not buy a ticket?" said the lady, smiling. "You might be the lucky man to get the prize."

"And what in the world would I do wi' a bride's-cake?" asked the Captain, his manly sailor's heart in a gentle palpitation. "Where would I get a bride to – to – to fit it?"

"I'm sure and I don't know," said the widow hurriedly, and she went on to explain the circumstances that had left it on her hands. The Captain listened attentively, eyed the elegant proportions of the cake in the window, and was seized by a desperate resolve.

"I never saw a finer bride's-cake," he said; "it's chust sublime! Do you think it would keep till the Gleska Fair?"

"It would keep a year for that part o't," said the widow. "What are you askin' that for?"

"If it'll keep to the Fair, and the Fair suits yoursel'," said Para Handy boldly, "we'll have it between us. What do you say to that, Mery?" and he leaned amorously over the counter.

"Mercy on me! this is no' the New Year time," exclaimed the widow; "I thought you never had any mind of me except at the New Year. Is this a proposal, Captain?"

"Don't caal me, Captain, caal me Peter, and gie me a haad o' your hand," entreated Para Handy languishingly.

"Well, then – Peter," murmured the widow, and the Captain went back to the *Vital Spark* that night an engaged man: the bride's-cake was withdrawn from the window, and the tortoise took up its quarters in the back shop.

Of all the ordeals Para Handy had to pass through before his marriage, there was none that troubled him more than his introduction to her relatives, and the worst of them was Uncle Alick, who was very old, very deaf, and very averse to his niece marrying again. The Captain and his "fiancée" visited him as in duty bound, and found him in a decidedly unfavourable temper. .

"This is Peter," said the widow by way of introduction; and the Captain stood awkwardly by her side, with his pea-jacket tightly buttoned to give him an appearance of slim, sprightly, and dashing youthfulness.

"What Peter?" asked the uncle, not taking his pipe out of his mouth, and looking with a cold, indifferent eye upon his prospective relative.

"You know fine," said the lady, flushing. "It's my lad."

"What did you say?" inquired Uncle Alick, with a hand behind his ear.

"My lad," she cried. "Peter Macfarlane – him that's Captain on the *Vital Spark.*"

"Catched him in a park," said Uncle Alick. "I'll wudger you didna need to run fast to catch him. Whatna park was it?"

"The *Fital Spark,*" roared the Captain, coming to Mary's assistance. "I'm captain on her."

"Are you, are you?" said Uncle Alick querulously. "Weel, you needna roar at me like that; I'm no' that deaf. You'll be wan o' the Macfarlanes from Achnatra; they were aal kind of droll in the mind, but hermless."

The Captain explained that he was a member of a different family altogether, but Uncle Alick displayed no interest in the explanation. "It's none of my business," said he.

"Mery thinks it is," rejoined the Captain. "That's the reason we're here."

"Beer!" said Uncle Alick. "No, no, I have no beer for you. I never keep drink of any sort in the hoose."

"I never said beer," exclaimed Para Handy.

"I'll be telling a lie then," said Uncle Alick. "The same ass if I didn't hear you with my own ears. You'll be the man that Mery's goin' to merry. I canna understand her; I'm sure she had plenty of trouble wi' Donald Crawford before he went and died on her. But it's none o' my business: I'm only an old done man, no' long for this world, and I'm not goin' to interfere wi' her if she wass to merry a bleck. She never consulted me, though I'm the only uncle she has. You shouldna put yoursel's to bother tellin' me anything aboot it; I'm sure I would have heard aboot it from some o' the neebours. The neebours iss very good to me. They're sayin' it's a droll-like thing Mery merryin' again, and her wi' a nice wee shop o' her own. What I says to them iss, 'It's her own business:

perhaps she sees something takin' in the man that nobody else does. Maybe,' I says to them, 'he'll give up his vessel and help her in the shop.' "

"Och, you're chust an old haiver!" remarked the Captain *sotto voce*, and of course the deaf man heard him.

"A haiver!" said he. "A nice-like thing to say aboot the only uncle Mery has, and him over eighty-six. But you're no' young yoursel'. Maybe it wass time for you to be givin' up the boats."

"I'm no' thinkin' o' givin' them up, Uncle," said Para Handy cheerfully. "The *Vital Spark's* the smertest boat in the tred. A bonny-like hand I would be in a shop. No, no, herself here – Mery, can keep the shop or leave it, chust ass it pleases hersel', it's aal wan to me; I'm quite joco. I hope you'll turn up at the weddin' on the fufteenth, for aal langsyne."

"What's your wull?" inquired Uncle Alick.

"I hope you'll turn up at the weddin' and give us support," bellowed the Captain.

"Give you sport," said the old man indignantly. "You'll surely get plenty of sport withoot takin' it off a poor old man like me."

"Och! to the muschief!" exclaimed the Captain somewhat impatiently. "Here's a half pound o' tobacco me and Mery brought you, and surely that'll put you in better trum."

"What wey did you no' say that at first?" said Uncle Alick. "Hoo wass I to know you werena wantin' the lend o' money for the weddin'? Stop you and I'll see if there's any spurits handy."

I was not at the wedding, but the Captain told me all about it some days afterwards. "It would be worth a bit in the papers," he said with considerable elation. "I'll wudger there wasna another weddin' like it in Kintyre for chenerations. The herrin' trawlers iss not back at their work yet, and herrin's up ten shullin's a box in Gleska. Dougie and The Tar and their wifes wass there, quite nate and tidy, and every noo and then Macphail would be comin' doon to the boat and blowin' her whustle. Och, he's not a bad chap Macphail, either, but chust stupid with readin' them novelles.

"I never saw Mery lookin' more majestic; she wass chust sublime! Some of them said I wassna lookin' slack mysel', and I daarsay no', for I wass in splendid trum. When the knot was tied, and we sat doon to a bite, I found it wass a different bride's-cake aalthegither from the wan that julted Cameron.

" 'What's the meanin' of that?' I whuspered to the mustress. 'That's no' the bride's-cake you had in the window.'

" 'No,' says she, 'but it's a far better one, isn't it?'

" 'It's a better-lookin' wan,' I says, 'but the other wan might have done the business.'

" 'Maybe it would,' she said, 'but I have all my wuts aboot me, and I wasna goin' to have the neighbours say that both the bride and bride's-cake were second-hand.' Oh! I'm tellin' you she's a smert wan the mustress!"

"Well, I wish you and your good lady long life and happiness, Captain," I said.

"Thanky, thanky," said he. "I'll tell the mustress. Could you no put a bit in the papers sayin', 'The rale and only belle o' Captain Macfarlane's weddin' wass the young lady first in the grand merch, dressed in broon silk.' "

"Who was the young lady dressed in brown?" I asked.

"What need you ask for?" he replied. "Who would it be but the mustress?"